THE MEN WHO FOUND AMERICA

This edition published 2024
by Living Book Press

ISBN: 978-1-76153-118-7 (hardcover)
         978-1-76153-119-4 (softcover)

First published in 1909.

This edition is based on the 1909 printing by Edward Stern & Co.

A catalogue record for this book is available from the National Library of Australia

THE MEN WHO FOUND AMERICA

by

FREDERICK WINTHROP HUTCHINSON

"COLUMBUS WAS DRESSED IN SHINING STEEL, WITH A BEAUTIFUL RED CLOAK, AND HE CARRIED THE RED AND YELLOW FLAG OF SPAIN."

CONTENTS

The Man Who Found America

More than four hundred years ago, when King Ferdinand and the wise, gentle Queen Isabella ruled over Spain, there came one day to the court, where the King and Queen and all the brave nobles and beautiful ladies stayed, a poor man named Christopher Columbus. He was poor, but he was very wise. He had a great plan, a plan to get heaps and heaps of shining pearls, and red rubies, and diamonds, and soft blue and white and yellow silks, and many other wonderful things for Spain and the good King and Queen. Columbus came to tell the King and Queen about his plan, and to ask them to help him.

In those days, even the wisest men believed that the earth was flat, like a table. They thought that if a ship sailed far, far across the wide ocean, it would fall off the edge of the earth, and down, down into a black hole that was so big and deep that it had no bottom. When Columbus was a little boy, he would often lie in the warm, sunny sands by the seashore and listen to the talk of the sailors, who came together and whispered stories of this far-off ocean. Once a sailor with long black hair and a big black beard told Christopher how his ship had sailed into a sea that was so hot that it sometimes boiled up like water in a tea-kettle. Another very big sailor, with only one eye, said that he had seen a big serpent gliding through the water, and ugly black demons who lay in wait for ships and men. Another sailor told of a bird as big as the tallest house. This bird lifted ships in its claws and dropped them down into the ocean with a great splash, and all the poor sailors were drowned. There was an old, old sailor who said that he had seen a big, black hand come up out of the sea and catch the ships and drag them down into the deep ocean. This sailor had a big, sharp knife in his belt. Once he whispered to little Christopher that he had sailed and sailed to the edge of the earth and had looked over the edge into the deep, black hole. And he said he was so frightened that his hair, that was as brown as a tree before, got quite white. He told little Christopher that this ocean was so terrible that people called it "The Sea of Darkness."

After many years little Christopher grew up to be a brave, wise man. He said, "These stories are foolish. They are not true." He had sailed often on the ocean and he had never seen the great black bird, or the big hand that came out of the sea, or any of these terrible things. He had read books, and he thought all night about the sea and the earth. "The earth has no edge," he said at last; "the earth is round."

One of the books that Columbus read was about a brave sailor named Marco Polo. This Marco Polo had gone far away from his little white house by the sea. He went always towards the rising sun, sometimes walking, sometimes riding on queer-looking camels with humps on their backs. The book told how Marco Polo had found in that far-off country beautiful, shining cities, with people in them who had never heard of God. This country was called the Indies. Marco Polo had brought home with him big white pearls and soft silks, and spices that smelled strange and sweet, and he said that anyone who could reach the Indies could get these beautiful things. But it took years and years to get there, and there were fierce robbers on the road, so the people were afraid to go.

Columbus, too, wanted to reach this wonderful land. But he knew an easier way than the long journey Marco Polo had taken. Columbus knew that the earth was round, like an orange, because he was very wise. And he said, "If it is round, then I can sail around it and I won't fall off the edge of the ocean, because there is no edge. So I will sail around the earth until I reach the Indies."

Then it was that Columbus went to the King and Queen and told them about his plan. The King and Queen were much surprised at the strange stories that Columbus told them, and they called around them their wise men to talk about it. The wise men of Spain laughed at Columbus. They said: "Columbus says the earth is round. If it is round, how do the people on the other side live? They would have to stand on their heads; the rain and snow would fall up instead of down; the sun would never shine there, and it would always be dark. People could not live like that." The wise men told the King and Queen not to help Columbus, because he was crazy. And the little boys and girls made fun of Columbus and touched their foreheads when he passed them in the streets, because their fathers had told them that Columbus was crazy.

So the King and Queen told Columbus that they would not help him. This made Columbus very sad. But he knew that he was right, and he kept on trying. He followed the King and Queen wherever they went. He went with them from city to city, always asking them for help. But there was a great war in Spain, and the King and Queen were too busy about the war to listen to Columbus.

At last Columbus said: "If the King and Queen of Spain will not help me, I will go to some other king and ask." He started to leave Spain. You can well believe that he was very sad. But then a very strange thing happened. On the way he stopped at a convent to beg some bread and water for his little son. This boy's name was Diego, which is the Spanish name for James. There was a good, wise old man at this convent. When he heard the story that Columbus told, he said he would help him. So the good old man from the convent went to see Queen Isabella and begged her to help Columbus. He told her how rich and great Spain would become if Columbus found the Indies. But still the Queen was afraid that Columbus was not right, and she said that she would not help him. Then Columbus was angry. He started again to leave Spain. This time he almost reached the end of Spain when he heard someone calling to him. It was a man sent by the Queen. "Good news! Good news!" cried the man. "Good Queen Isabella has promised to help you. She has said: 'I will give Columbus ships and men, even if I must sell my golden crown and my beautiful rings and chains to get the money.'"

How glad Columbus was! He had waited a long, long time, and now, at last, he could go on his voyage. Queen Isabella gave him three ships, and sailors to sail them, and she told Columbus that if he found the golden Indies she would give him barrels of shining gold and some of the pearls and diamonds and silks that he would find there. Columbus thanked her and kissed her hand, which is the way people do with Queens. The King and Queen and all the great lords, with their shining swords and velvet coats, and the pretty ladies came down to sea to say good-by to Columbus, and he sailed away into the big, strange ocean.

For many days Columbus sailed and sailed and sailed. At first the sailors with him were happy and obedient, for Columbus said, "I will give you lots of beautiful things when we reach the Indies." But as they sailed day after day into this strange ocean, they grew very, very much afraid. At night, when Columbus could not see them, they got together and whispered to each other stories of the big black hand that pulled ships down into the sea, and of the great bird that lifted ships high into the air and then dropped them deep into the ocean, so that the poor sailors were drowned. Even the soft, gentle wind that blew always from the east frightened them. "How can we ever get back to Spain," they cried, "if the wind blows always away from Spain?" For in those days they had no steamers, with big engines that can send ships anywhere. They had only ships with sails, which went the way the wind blew.

At last the sailors begged Columbus to go back. "We shall all die in this strange sea," they cried, "and we shall never see our wives and little babies. Let us go back." But Columbus would not go back. Every day he told them stories of the rich, beautiful country which they would find. And he told them to be brave. But after a while they would not listen any more; and when they found that Columbus would not go back, some of them said: "Let us throw Columbus into the sea. Then we can go back to Spain, and if any one asks us, 'Where is Columbus?' we will say that he fell into the ocean." Columbus knew what they said, but he was brave and was not afraid. He believed that if he sailed far enough he would reach the beautiful Indies.

Then, one day, they saw something on the far-off ocean, and the sailors joyfully shouted, "Land! Land!" But when they sailed near, they saw it was only a cloud. Then the sailors were sad again. Every day they all looked out for land. Queen Isabella had promised a handful of shining gold to the one who first saw land, and Columbus said he would also give a fine velvet coat.

How lonely the poor sailors were! Every day they saw nothing but the wide, wide ocean, with the rolling waves. At last, one day, some birds flew over the ships. "Look! Look!" the sailors shouted joyfully. And they said, "If there are birds, there must be land for them to rest on." But although they looked and looked, and sailed quickly after the birds, they could not find land.

Then, on another day, Columbus fished out of the sea a hawthorn branch with berries on it, and a carved stick. The sailors crowded around to look at the branch and the stick, and laughed and sang for joy. "There must be land for the hawthorn to grow on," they said, "and there must be people who carved this stick." Everyone was glad and happy and watched eagerly for land.

Columbus watched too. One night he stood alone on his ship, looking out over the black ocean. All at once he saw a little light in the darkness. It was so little he could not be sure it was a light. So he called two of his men and asked them whether they could see the light. "Yes! yes!" they cried, "we can see it. It seems to move up and down." Still, they could not be quite sure until, about two hours afterwards, when the morning began to grow brighter, one of the other ships fired a gun. This meant that they had seen land.

When the sun came up, everyone could see the land. It was a beautiful land, with waving green trees and flowers. But it seemed even more beautiful than it really was to brave Columbus and his poor, tired sailors, because they had seen nothing but the wide ocean for so many days. They quickly rowed their boats to the shore and landed. Columbus was dressed in shining steel, with a beautiful red cloak, and he carried the red and yellow flag of Spain. His captains also carried flags. They all knelt down on the shore and thanked God for bringing them to this beautiful place.

They did not see any of the beautiful cities that Marco Polo had written about, but men came out of the woods and ran up to them on the beach. These men had straight black hair and brown skins, with bright-colored feathers in their hair, and they had hardly any clothes on. "Look! Look at the people from heaven!" they cried, when they saw Columbus and his men, with their white skins and beautiful clothes, and their ships, which looked like big white birds. These people were Indians—not fierce like the Indians we know, but very kind and gentle. Columbus had never seen an Indian before, and the Indians had never seen a white man in all their lives. So both Columbus and the Indians were very much surprised and looked at each other for a long time. Columbus was very kind to the Indians. He gave them little red caps and pretty glass beads and little tinkling bells. The Indians liked these things very much, and they gave Columbus fresh fruits and beautiful red and green parrots and little bits of gold.

Columbus called these people Indians because he thought this country was part of the Indies that Marco Polo had written about. He did not know that he had discovered a wonderful new world, far richer and more beautiful than the golden Indies. This new world was our own America, the beautiful land where we all live now.

After a while, Columbus went back to Spain to tell the King and Queen about this land. When Columbus sailed up to the city by the sea, the people in Spain cheered and rang bells and fired guns to show their joy. When Columbus came to the throne, the King and Queen made him sit down beside them. This was a great honor, because no one is allowed to sit down when a king or queen is in the room. So Columbus sat down and told them how he had sailed across the Sea of Darkness and at last found this beautiful country. How glad now was the good Queen Isabella that she had sent Columbus! She made him a great lord in Spain and gave him gold and jewels; and she kept his little son Diego always with her, to hold up her long silken train and to carry her fan and handkerchief.

Columbus was happy now. But he wanted to see more of this new land, and he sailed across the ocean again three times. Once, while he was away, some wicked men told the King and Queen lies about Columbus. The King and Queen believed what these wicked men said, and they ordered their soldiers to put big iron chains on Columbus' hands and feet and send him back to Spain. Poor Columbus! How sad he felt! When they came to Spain and Columbus saw Queen Isabella, she soon found that he was a good man and that the stories about him were not true, and she told the soldiers to take the chains off Columbus, and said she was sorry. But Columbus was still sad, because after he had found this beautiful country for Spain, they had put chains on him. So he always kept the chains, and when he died, he asked the people to bury the chains with him.

There was another thing that happened that was not fair to Christopher Columbus. When a man finds a new country, it always ought to be named after him. But our country was never called Columbia. About seven years after Columbus found the new country, an Italian, named Amerigo Vespucci, sailed across the ocean and wrote a little book about the new land. He did not say one word about Christopher Columbus being there first. So many foolish people thought that Amerigo was the man who found the new country, and they called it America, in honor of Amerigo. And this is its name to-day; and this, I think, will always be its name.

Columbus was old when he died, and he was poor, too. Good, kind Queen Isabella had died, and the King forgot that Columbus had found a beautiful new country for him, and he did not give him any more money. So Columbus was sad and poor. After he was dead the people knew that the country he had found was not the Indies, but a rich, wonderful country, our own America. And that is why all good Americans love the name of Christopher Columbus, because he came and found America.

THE WHITE TYRANT OF DARIEN

Christopher Columbus was not only a brave man, he was also a very good man. I wish that I could say the same of all the Spaniards who came after him. But many of these men were cruel and deceitful and wicked. They were not kind to the Indians, and they fought and robbed and cheated, and their only thought was to grow rich.

Now, one of the most wicked of all these Spaniards was Balboa. His full name was Vasco Nuñez de Balboa, but I think I shall call him only Balboa. He was as cruel as a man could be. He liked to see people suffer, and if anyone was in trouble, Balboa would not help him, but would laugh at the poor man's misfortune. He borrowed money and promised to pay it back; but when the time came, he told the people who had lent him the money to get it back the best way they could. He quarreled with everybody, and everybody said that he was a wicked, wicked man.

This Balboa was born in Spain; but like many other Spaniards, he went to America to live. Now there was in America a great island called Hispaniola, where many Spaniards had houses. These Spaniards were very cruel to the kind, gentle Indians. They made slaves of them, and they made them work so very hard and so very long that many of the poor Indians died. And all the while the Spaniards lived without doing any work themselves. They walked about in their fine clothes, and they drank and swore and quarreled with one another, and in every way were as bad as bad could be. And of all these wicked Spaniards, Balboa was the worst. Whenever anything wicked was to be done, Balboa would do it. You see he was not only wicked, but very brave and very, very bold.

Well, after a while, Balboa grew tired of the lazy life in Hispaniola. He wanted to become rich, and it was harder to get money in Hispaniola than in other parts of America. Besides, nobody in all the island liked Balboa. He was so cruel and quarrelsome, so unkind to the Indians, that the people used to look at him coldly, and shake their heads when they passed him in the street. Then, too, those who had lent money to him began to want it back again, and some men said to Balboa, "If you do not pay back the money you owe us, we shall throw you into prison, and there you can stay in the dark with the rats and the mice until you die." For in those cruel days, a man who could not pay his debts was thrown into prison. Now, you can well believe that the wicked Balboa was only too anxious to get away from the island. But how could he do it? He could not walk away, because an island has water on all sides, and he could not go by boat, because he had no money; so he thought and thought and thought. And at last Balboa hit upon a very clever plan. One day he walked down to the sea-coast, where a ship was being loaded, and when nobody was watching he quickly crawled into a great empty wine-cask and pulled the lid on the top. There he waited and waited, hour after hour, afraid every moment that someone would miss him and look in the wine-casks on the boat. He hardly dared breathe, and even the beating of his heart seemed to him as loud as a great drum.

But no one came, and at last the boat took up its anchor and sailed away. Then Balboa was very happy, for he knew that he was free from Hispaniola and all the people who hated him and all the people to whom he owed money. He knew that he would not have to go to prison. But at first he was afraid to come out of the cask, because he was afraid of what the captain would say when he saw him. He waited a good many hours in the barrel, but at last he gave a shove to the lid, and out popped the red face and red beard of Balboa. As he did so, he heard the captain and all the sailors give a great shout, for you may be sure that they were much surprised to see a man's head come out of a barrel.

Now, the captain, whose name was Encisco, was a very disagreeable man, and he was quite angry when he saw Balboa's head come out of the barrel. He did not like to carry people on his ship for nothing, and he thought that Balboa had cheated him when he hid himself in a barrel. "What does this mean?" he shouted, and then he swore so many oaths that I am glad you and I were not there, though perhaps we could not have understood, because it was all in Spanish.

Well, when Balboa told the captain how he had to run away from the island, and how he had no money to pay for the voyage, Encisco became angrier and angrier. He stamped his foot and shook his fist; his eyes got black, and he swore and swore and swore. "I will tell you what I will do with you," roared the captain so loud that the wicked Balboa shook with fear; "I shall put you on a desert island without food or water and you can starve to death, you wicked cheater."

Now, I must say that Balboa was a brave man, but at these cruel words he became very frightened. He knew that Encisco would do as he said. In those days people did not think much about killing each other, and Balboa was so cruel himself that he would have treated the captain just as cruelly as the captain was now going to treat him; so Balboa threw himself on his knees and begged the captain to spare his life. He begged and begged, but the more he begged, the more the captain swore and the angrier he grew. But at last, he did feel a *little* sorry for Balboa; so he said, "Get up from your knees. This time I will spare your life." Now, you will think, perhaps, that Balboa was very grateful to the captain for sparing his life, but really he was not. He kissed the captain's hand and thanked him over and over again, and swore that he would lay down his life for Encisco whenever he wished it; but in his real secret heart he hated the captain and only waited for the chance to do him harm.

Well, the chance came sooner even than Balboa had thought. One day a great storm came up and the little ship tossed and rocked and everybody was afraid that the boat would go down. The sailors, who were wicked men, went down on their knees and tried to pray that their lives might be spared. But they had all forgotten how to say their prayers, and the storm grew worse and worse, and at last the little ship was dashed to pieces on a rocky coast. The sailors all fell into the sea, but luckily for them the water was not deep and they were able to swim ashore alive. At last the men were all on land again, but not one of them knew the name of the place or the name of the country where they had been wrecked. They looked up and down the coast, but everywhere they found only sand and rocks, and back a little way great woods of waving palm-trees.

Now the captain ought always to know where he takes his ship; so each of the sailors asked the captain the name of the country. But the captain had never been in any of that country, and he did not know the name any better than the sailors; so you may well believe that they were all very much frightened. Then up spoke the crafty Balboa. He had been very quiet and respectful on the boat, because he was still afraid of the desert island; but here on the land he was as bold as you please. "Captain," he said, "I know where we are, for I have been here before. This is the country of Darien, and a little way off is an Indian village to which I will take you."

Now, when the sailors heard these words of Balboa, they were very glad. They cheered and cheered and threw up their caps, which were still wet from the sea-water. Then they all started off for the Indian village, everybody following bold Balboa, and if you had looked on at this strange march, you would have thought that Balboa was the real captain and Encisco only a sailor. It was not easy to march through this country of Darien, because the Indians were very unfriendly. You see, before this time some other Spaniards had come to the country, and robbed and killed and tortured the Indians.

Perhaps Balboa was one of these very men. Well, anyway, the Indians did not love the white men who had been so cruel, and so from behind trees they shot arrows at the ship-wrecked sailors. Many sailors were killed and more were wounded; but Balboa, though very wicked, was a brave and wise General, and he beat off the Indians and got the sailors safely to the little Indian village.

At last the time had come for Balboa to make Captain Encisco sorry for wanting to put him off on a desert island. You see Balboa could never forgive the captain for making him kneel and beg for his life. Besides, he was very proud and wanted all the glory for himself. So Balboa took the sailors aside one by one, and whispered to each of them, "Encisco is a poor captain and I am a good one. Make me your captain and I will treat you better than Encisco does." So the sailors all made Balboa their captain.

Now, at last, Balboa had his wish and was a great man in a new country. Here he could get money and become very rich; but I am sorry to say that he was always very, very cruel. He used to rob the poor Indians and murder them, and when they did not have as much gold as he wanted, he would tie them up by their thumbs until they screamed with pain. He made them hang there until they told him where more gold could be found. Sometimes the poor Indians would not know; but just to be rid of the pain, they would pretend that gold was hidden in the forest and they would take Balboa to the place. But if Balboa did not find any gold there, and often he did not, it went still worse with the poor Indians. He would burn them alive on a slow fire, so that they would suffer great pain. Indeed, he grew so cruel that the Indians called him "The White Tyrant of Darien."

One day the son of an Indian chief came to where Balboa was living and spoke to the tyrant. "You always want gold," said he, "but I will show you something still better. Come with me a few days to the West, and you may see an ocean as great as the great sea you sailed when you came from your home." Now, Balboa thought, "If I can find this great sea and be the first white man to look at it, then I shall be a famous man. Besides, there may be gold and silver and jewels in the lands beyond this new sea." So off he went, taking with him the chief's son and some of the Spanish sailors. It was not a long journey, and in a few days they came to a mountain. This the Indian told Balboa to climb. "From the top," he said, "you will see the great ocean."

Balboa told all his men to stay below, and he went up alone to the top of the mountain; and what the Indian had said came true. There lay the great sea, stretching in all directions as far as the eye could reach. The blue waters were as quiet as a little lake; but Balboa knew that this was a great ocean. And it *was* a great ocean—the Pacific Ocean, which is the greatest body of water in the world. So Balboa, who had run away from Hispaniola and had hidden himself in a barrel, was the first white man to see it.

Then Balboa, wicked and cruel though he was, knelt down on the top of the mountain and thanked God that he had been the first to see this great ocean. After that he called up his men. Up they ran, each trying to be the first, and when they reached the top, they all looked with wonder at the great, peaceful sea, that shone so beautifully in the noonday sun.

Then the men piled up great stones until there was a high heap, and Balboa went down the mountain and carved the name of King Ferdinand upon the bark of the trees. A few days later Balboa came down the mountain to the sea, which before he had only seen, but not touched. He walked a little way out into the ocean, and, waving his sword in the air, cried out in a loud voice that all that great sea and all the islands in it and all the lands about it belonged to Ferdinand, the King of Spain.

Now, if any one did such a foolish thing to-day, I believe that we would all laugh at him. A great ocean cannot belong to any one man, even if he is a King, or even to any one nation, but to all the nations and all the people of the world. But King Ferdinand was very proud when he heard of what the bold Balboa had done, and so he made him the ruler of the great ocean he had found.

But the wicked Balboa did not go without punishment for all his evil deeds. Every day he became more hard and more cruel. He did not keep his promise to be kinder than Encisco, and everybody hated him, even the people who knew that he was brave. So one day the Governor of Darien had him sent to prison, and a short time after that Balboa's head was cut off.

I do not know that anybody was sorry. Balboa was a very brave, bold man, and he *did* find the Pacific Ocean. But the braver a man is, the more gentle and kind and good he should be; so I think Balboa deserved his death, just as he deserved the name the Indians had given him of "The White Tyrant of Darien."

THE BEAUTIFUL CITY OF
THE FLOATING ISLANDS

Columbus had gone on his great journey to find gold, but nowhere did he find it. Other Spaniards came to America, all looking for gold, like Columbus. But gold does not grow in the street nor on the dusty roads. It is found in gold mines, deep, deep under the earth, where men work by candle-light and dig and dig.

Now, there was a man named Cortez, who wanted gold—much gold. He wanted to become a very rich man and go back to Spain, and live in a beautiful castle, with servants, and horses, and fine clothes, and jewels of many colors that glistened in the sun. Cortez was a very young man when he went to America to live. He was only nineteen, but he was strong and as brave as a lion. There was a Spanish Governor in the island where Cortez lived, and the Governor did not like Cortez. He threw the young man into prison, and when Cortez escaped, the Governor threw him in again. But Cortez was very brave and very clever, and so once more he got away, and hid himself so that the Governor could not find him.

Now, there had come news from further west, from the land which we now call Mexico, that there was much gold in that land. So the Governor of the island said to himself, "I will send some soldiers there, and they will take the gold away from the Indians and bring it to me; then I shall be a rich man, and can go back to Spain and live in a castle." For in those days there were castles in Spain, large and gray and beautiful, with great iron gates and a ditch of water all around, so that no man could enter except the friends of the owner. You see the Governor of this island wanted to be rich and great, and that is why he sent a little army of Spanish soldiers to the new land of Mexico.

"Who is the man that will lead my army?" asked the Governor. "There will be many dangers. Perhaps the ships will go down in a storm and all will be drowned; perhaps the food will give out and the soldiers and their Generals will die from hunger, or it may be that the Indians will fight them and shoot them to death with bows and arrows. I must have a good General—strong, and as brave as a lion." And then he thought of Cortez, the brave, strong young Spaniard, and he made him General of the little army.

So one day the ships sailed away to the new land of Mexico. Cortez cheered the men by telling them stories of the great country they were going to find. "We are to sail and to fight," said he; "to fight for our good King, for Spain and for God. The people that live in this land are not Christians. They do not believe in our God, and we must teach them about Him and make them Christians." But even while he spoke, the young Cortez thought of gold, gold, gold—dollars of gold piled up to the sky; goblets and plates and dishes of gold; tables and chairs of gold. Gold, gold, yellow gold, that would make the young Spaniard the richest man in all the world.

The little ships took up their anchors and sailed west towards the sun setting in the waters. It was a beautiful sea, all green and blue, with here and there reefs of white coral, and at last, far in the distance, they saw the beautiful new land of Mexico. The sun shone bright upon the green trees of the forest, and all the flowers of the field, red and purple and blue and yellow, glistened in the bright light. The boats came up to the shore. "Here," cried Cortez, as he stood on the white beach, "here I shall found my city, and I shall call it the 'City of the True Cross,' in honor of God and the good King of Spain." And to this day the city bears that name—the "City of the True Cross."

Now, there lived in the new land of Mexico, high up behind the mountains, a nation of Indians called Aztecs. They were very proud and strong and brave, and had conquered many peoples. These Aztecs were not like the Indians we see in the circus. They had a beautiful city made of wood and stone, with houses full of gold and silver ornaments, and this wonderful city was built upon floating islands. The King of the Aztecs was a very great man. His name was Montezuma, and his father had been King before him and his grandfather had been King before *him*; and so, for so many, many years, that no one among the Aztecs, even the oldest, could remember.

Now, there was a story among the Aztecs that some day the Children of the Sun would come from the East and drive Montezuma and his Indians away. These Children of the Sun, according to the story, were not red like the Aztecs, but white like Cortez and his Spanish soldiers. So when Montezuma heard of the white men, who had come and founded the City of the True Cross, he called his wise men together. They were very old and very wise, and they bowed deep to Montezuma, because he was King, and they listened to what he said.

"Now, my Lords," said Montezuma to the wise men about him, "I have strange news to tell you. There have come from the East the Children of the Sun. They are white men, with black hair and beards, and their clothes are made of metal as bright as silver, so that it glistens in the sun. They ride on big, strong animals that run faster than a man." You see, Montezuma had never seen horses. "And," went on the King, "these children have come here in houses that sail on the sea—in ships such as we Aztecs know not of. I fear that, when they see our beautiful city, they will kill our people, and then the Aztec nation will be no more."

The King paused, and in the great hall, where the wise men were gathered, all was silent, so silent that the breathing of the wise men could be heard. Then again the King spoke:

"My Lords!" he called out, "what shall I do?"

And a young man, the bravest of all the Aztec princes, arose quietly and, facing the King, answered his question.

"The Aztecs, my Lord," he said, "have always fought. We must do as our fathers have ever done, fight for our King and our beautiful 'City of the Floating Islands.'"

Montezuma was silent as he listened to the brave words of the young prince, and all the wise men were silent too.

Then a very old man, the oldest and wisest of all the wise

"THE KIND KING MONTEZUMA WANTED PEACE, AND SAID THAT HE WOULD GIVE THE SPANIARDS MORE GOLD IF THEY WOULD ONLY GO BACK TO THEIR OWN COUNTRY."

men in the kingdom, rose in his turn; and all the wise men listened as the old man spoke.

"Not so, my gracious King, not so," he said slowly. "We are brave men, but we cannot fight the Children of the Sun. It is true that our soldiers are many and the white men are few; but the Sun has given to them his fire. They have tubes that are called guns, and when the Indians fight these white children, the tubes speak out fire and noise, which kill the red men. Where are our brothers to the East who have fought the white men? Dead, my Lord, dead. We cannot fight against the Sun or against his children. We must send to the white men presents—rich presents of gold and silver, and beg them to go away in their houses that sail the sea—to go away, they, and their horses, and their guns, and not come up to our beautiful city."

And as the old man had said, so the King Montezuma did. He gathered together great chests of gold and silver, dresses and cloaks of bright green peacock feathers, and heaps and heaps of red rubies, and milky white pearls, and precious jewels that glistened in the sun. "Take these to the white men," he said to his servants; "take this gold and silver and all these beautiful gifts to the white men, who are Children of the Sun, and beg them to go away and not come up to our beautiful city."

The servants did as Montezuma had bidden them. They did not have horses, but all day and all night they ran as swift as the bird flies, until at last they came to where Cortez and his soldiers waited. Then they fell on their knees and bowed their heads to the ground.

"Behold, oh Children of the Sun," they said, "this gold and silver, and all these rubies and precious stones, and all these beautiful things are the presents of our good King Montezuma to the white men who have come from the East; and our King Montezuma begs the white men not to go up to his beautiful city, but to take the gold and silver and to go away in their wonderful houses that sail on the sea."

Now, when Cortez saw all the gold and silver that Montezuma had sent, he became very greedy. He wanted still more gold, and he knew that if Montezuma could send him such beautiful presents, there must be great riches in the wonderful city. So he said to the waiting servants, "Tell your good King Montezuma that I thank him for the gold and silver which he has sent me, and that I and all my men with me will come to visit him in his beautiful city."

Then the servants went back with the message. Now, it was a long and dangerous journey to the beautiful city of the Aztecs, and Cortez feared that his men might be afraid to go so far from their ships, so he called them together. "I am going on a long and dangerous journey," he said; "those who go with me shall become rich, very rich, but those who are afraid can stay here on the seacoast." And the soldiers answered, "You are our General, Cortez, and where you go we will go too." Then Cortez burned his ships so that no one could turn back, and with his little army marched up to the beautiful city where King Montezuma lived.

Now, when Montezuma heard that the white men were coming to his beautiful city, he did not know what to do. Some of his wise men said, "Let us fight the Children of the

Sun," and others said, "Let us have peace; let us welcome the white men as guests to our city." So Montezuma did not know what to do.

When Cortez reached the high lands and looked out upon the city, he saw the strangest sight in the world. The city was built on islands that floated on the lakes, and there was water all about it, and bridges with gates, and soldiers that stood by the gates to keep the white men out. And Cortez was afraid. You see the bridges were very narrow, and it would have been very easy for the Aztecs to shoot the Spanish soldiers as they crossed the bridges; so the crafty Cortez said to the Indians, "Listen, my friends; let us come into your beautiful City of the Floating Islands, for we are tired after our long journey. Let us rest with you a little, for we are your friends and we wish you to be ours."

So the Aztecs let the white men cross the bridges and enter the gates of their city. Now, as soon as Cortez and his soldiers were inside the city they behaved very badly. They went out on the streets and quarreled with the Aztecs. They found fault with the palace, which the good King Montezuma had given them to live in, and they always thought of ways in which to take from the Aztecs their gold and silver and precious stones. Now, Cortez, who was very strong and brave, was also very cruel and deceitful. He invited Montezuma to come and see him in his palace, and when the Aztec King came to see him, Cortez told his soldiers to hold him prisoner. Then the white men went out into the streets and fought the good Indians and killed many of them. The kind King Montezuma wanted peace, and said that he would give the Spaniards more gold if they would only go back to their own country. But the Spaniards did not wish to go back, not until they had found all the gold and silver in all the land of the Aztecs. So they fought battles, many battles, and the Spaniards, who were brave, but very, very cruel, conquered all that country. Many of the Aztecs were killed, and even the good King Montezuma lost his life.

Thus it all came to pass just as the wise men had foretold, and the City of the Floating Islands became the white men's city.

But it did not go well with Cortez. To be sure, at first he became very rich, and had beautiful houses, and lands, and horses, and gold and silver; but he did not long keep these things. He grew poor again, and when he got to be an old man, he was very sad and unhappy. And sometimes I think he must have been sorry for his cruelties, and lies, and wickedness, and for all the unkind things he did to the poor Aztecs when he and his soldiers went up into Mexico and conquered the beautiful City of the Floating Islands.

THE SWINEHERD WHO
WANTED A CASTLE

Once upon a time, there lived in a little village in Spain a boy who tended pigs. He was a very ragged boy. His clothes were old and torn; he wore no cap, and he had never in all his life had on a pair of shoes. His food was even worse than his clothing. He ate nuts and grapes and stale crusts of bread, and sometimes he had cheese. But meat he could not have more than once a month. This was because the boy was very, very poor.

Now, it is not pleasant to tend pigs. They are *such* dirty animals, and they grunt and grunt and make ugly noises all the time. It is very disagreeable to sit all day and have nothing to do but to talk to filthy pigs, and see that they do not walk off into the woods and get lost. So the little Spanish boy hated his work and wished that he could get away.

The name of this little boy was Francisco Pizarro. I do not wish to pretend that he was a good boy, because he was not. He was a bad boy, and he grew up to be a wicked man; but one thing I must say for him, he was surely very brave. And perhaps he became bad because, as a boy, he did not have a good home nor any nice boys to play with.

Near where Francisco lived was a beautiful castle. It had big, light rooms, and long tables, and fine gilt chairs, and wonderful pictures, and everything that the heart could desire. Francisco had never seen the inside of this castle. There was a great wall all around it, and in this wall a big, strong gate that was locked every night. A soldier in a yellow-and-red coat stood at this gate, and of course he would not let the ragged little swineherd in. The young Francisco used to watch the old soldier as he pulled at his mustache, and sometimes, when the soldier wasn't looking, the boy pressed his head against the iron bars and looked into the garden. He could only see a little corner of the castle, but he saw the beautiful trees in the garden, and the soft, green grass and the fountain which seemed so cool in the hot afternoons.

It made Francisco very angry to see this beautiful garden and not be allowed to go into it. He complained to his mother, but she could not do anything, because it wasn't her castle, and she was as poor as Francisco. "You are only a swineherd," she said to him, "and swineherds cannot have castles; so stop thinking of the castle and go back to your pigs."

But Francisco did not stop thinking of the castle. He had seen in the garden a little boy of his own age, and he saw that the boy's clothes were made of fine, soft cloth, and that he had a lovely black feather in his cap. He remembered, too, that a kind old man, with a long white beard, had walked with this boy in the garden, and had taught him many things out of a great book. Poor Francisco had never been to school, and he had never had a teacher, like this boy with the fine clothes; but he wanted all the things that the little boy in the garden had, and he made up his mind that he would get them.

I told you before that Francisco was not a good boy, and so he did not ask himself whether it was right for him to want all these things. "I do not care," he said almost out loud; "I do not care what my mother says, or what the priest says, or anybody. Good or bad, right or wrong, I am going to get my castle." That will show you the sort of a boy Francisco really was.

Now, Francisco saw that it was no use to stay in his little village; there he would always be a swineherd. Every day he hated the pigs more and more. He hated them so much that he threw stones at them when they squealed. At last, with two other boys, he ran away. I think that Francisco and his two friends were a little afraid, at first, that their mothers would send after them and catch them. So they went away by night, and by the next morning they were far along the quiet road. Day after day they walked. They used to find chestnuts on the ground, and over the high, green hedges hung bunches of wild purple grapes that anybody might pick. The good country people were all as poor as poor could be; but they always gave the tired boys a bite of bread and a cup of goat's milk. Francisco was very happy. He was glad to be away from the dirty, squealing pigs, and he believed that every step he took brought him nearer to the castle he had dreamed of.

At last, the boys reached Seville. Now, Seville was a very large and beautiful city. There were fine houses and glorious palaces, like the castle that Francisco wanted, and women in beautiful dresses and men rode up and down the crowded streets on great black horses. It was all like Wonderland; and, as Francisco looked at everything—the streets, shops and people—his eyes almost popped out of his head.

But in this rich city of Seville, Francisco was poorer than ever before in all his life. Here in the great city nobody cared for the ragged boy, and there were no kind country people to give him bread and goat's milk. Yet, after a while, Francisco managed to make a little money, though even then he was still poor. Often he went to bed without supper, and his castle seemed to be as far away as ever.

Of all the things in the great city of Seville, Francisco liked the soldiers best. They seemed so big and brave in their beautiful uniforms, and the boy envied them and wished that he, too, could be a soldier. "It's a good way to get rich," he thought to himself. It *was* a good way in those times. Nowadays people don't get rich by killing each other; but in the olden days, to be a soldier was one of the best ways to get money and become great.

So Pizarro, who was now quite big and strong, became a soldier. A great war was being fought in Italy, and Pizarro was sent there with other Spanish soldiers to fight for his King. The young man was very brave. I think that, even then, he was cruel, but the Spaniards did not care about that, so long as he was only brave. So when he came back from the great war in Italy, everybody said "Pizarro is a very good soldier."

Now, in the meantime, Columbus had found America. I told you in another story, how the people in Spain were very glad over the news, and how everybody wanted to go to the wonderful new lands to make a fortune. Well, you may be sure that Pizarro wanted to go too; but for a long time he could not leave Spain. I cannot tell you why, because I do not know myself. Anyhow, he could not. But at last he got a chance, and with a band of other Spaniards went to the new country that Columbus had found.

By this time Pizarro was no longer a boy, nor even a young man; he was almost forty years of age. He had seen many lands and done many things; yet he was still poor, and it seemed to him as though the castle that he had dreamed of as a boy was as far away as ever.

Well, at first America was no better than Spain. Pizarro lived on a rich island, which was then named Hispaniola, but which is now called Cuba. There were many other Spaniards on the island, and these were all just as greedy and anxious to get rich as Pizarro. They were a very wicked set of men. All the bad things that a man can do they did; but above all, they were cruel to the poor Indians. They used to make the red men work for them day and night, and if the work was not enough, they beat the poor Indians until they died. I think that Pizarro was just as cruel as the rest; but in spite of his wickedness he did not get rich.

Now, after a while, when Pizarro was almost fifty years old, he went to a new country in America, where the Indians were very rich, and where there were very few Spaniards. This was the land of Darien, where Balboa had gone about ten years before. Here the friendly Indians had much gold and many beautiful jewels. They gave to Pizarro many precious stones and more gold than he had had in all his life; so the swineherd became rich at last.

But Pizarro was not satisfied even with these riches. The

"IF YOU WILL LET ME GO FREE, PIZARRO, I WILL FILL UP THIS ROOM WITH GOLD, AND IT WILL ALL BE YOURS."

more he had, the more he wanted; so one day, when he heard of some islands in the great ocean to the West, where the Indians were very rich, he made up his mind to go to these islands and take the gold from these Indians. His men were very glad to go, so they got canoes and paddled out to where the islands lay. This was a very bold thing to do, because the sea was rough, and many times the canoes turned over and the soldiers were almost drowned.

At last they reached the island, and Pizarro, standing up in his canoe, saw the Indians crowding on the beach, with their bows and arrows in hand, ready to shoot the first Spaniard who landed. Now, Pizarro, though a wicked and greedy man, was very brave; so he told his soldiers to fire their guns. As soon as the Indians heard the guns of the Spaniards they were frightened, and after a little battle they ran away. Then Pizarro and his men landed on the sandy beach. Here they found many pearls, which they took, and when there were no more pearls on the island, they paddled back to their homes.

When Pizarro had sold these pearls he was very rich indeed. He had now enough money to buy his castle. It was really not *exactly* a castle, but a fine, big house in Darien, with fields around it and cattle, and a great many Indian servants to do whatever Pizarro wanted. You would think *now* that Pizarro would be satisfied, for he was a hundred times richer than the other little boy who used to live in the castle in the old, old days when Pizarro was only a swineherd.

But the greedy Pizarro was *never* satisfied. After a few years, he heard how the brave Cortez had conquered Mexico, and he heard, too, that Cortez had become even richer than he was. So Pizarro wanted to be as rich as Cortez, and he looked around for a new nation to conquer.

Now, at this time there was living in Peru, many hundreds of miles to the South, a great tribe of Indians called the Incas. They were not savages, but wise, kind people like the Aztecs of Mexico, whom Cortez had conquered. These Incas were very rich. They had wonderful gold and silver mines, and they owned so much gold and silver that they could cover walls with them; and they also had precious stones, green emeralds, red rubies, blue sapphires and beautiful, brilliant diamonds that glistened in the sun.

I could tell you many things about these curious people—how they prayed to the sun and the moon instead of to God; of the wonderful temples and palaces that they built; of their fine, hard roads cut through the mountains, and of the King's messengers, who ran along these roads, day and night, carrying news. I could tell you how all the people obeyed the Inca, who was King of the country; how they all worked for him, and how he gave them food and clothing and houses, so that no man in all the land was ever hungry or thirsty or cold.

Now, when Pizarro heard of these Incas, he thought to himself, "I will go up to Peru and fight with these people, and take away from them all their gold and silver and jewels and all their cities and palaces." I think that it was wicked of Pizarro to want to disturb these good, quiet people, and it seems to me that the man who had been a poor swineherd should have been satisfied with the money he had, and could have left the Incas alone.

But Pizarro was always greedy. He got together a little band of soldiers and started to go up to Peru. I say up, because Peru was high up among the mountains. Pizarro thought that it would be easy to find Peru; but things did not go as he had hoped. Nobody could tell him where the great country lay, and there were no maps to show him the way. By mistake, Pizarro and his little army landed on a lonely desert island in the Pacific Ocean. There were swamps and marshes on this island, and there was little to eat, and even the water was not good to drink. The men suffered from mosquitoes and great flies, that stung them so they could not sleep. And worse than all, there were poisonous snakes that bit the men so that they died. They suffered from hunger and thirst, and some fell sick and died. Pizarro sent back his ship for more men and more food, and I am sure he was glad when, after a few weeks, the white sails were seen again. The ship brought plenty of food; but the Governor, of Darien, who was jealous of Pizarro, would not send any more soldiers. Instead, he sent word by the ship to Pizarro, saying, "Pizarro, you must come back to Darien."

Now, the men were only too glad to go back. They had suffered enough, and they did not want to be bitten and starved any more—no, not for a hundred Perus. "We will go home," they said, "as our Governor says." At first the bold Pizarro said nothing; then with the point of his sword he drew a sharp line in the sand.

"North of this line," he said, "is home; south of this line are Peru and glory and gold." And then he stepped across the line, meaning that *he* was going to Peru, even if he had to go alone. The soldiers all saw that Pizarro was a brave man, but none of them wanted to go with him. "We do not wish to be killed," they said to themselves. At last, the pilot of the ship, a brave, reckless fellow, with a long beard, name Luiz, crossed the line. "I go," he said, "wherever Pizarro leads." After that others followed. At last there were thirteen men across the line who were willing to go with Francisco Pizarro.

These brave men, I can tell you, had a pretty hard time before they reached Peru. They had to cross the sea on a raft, which is a very dangerous thing to do. But the Indians were kind to them and gave them food to eat, and when they got to Peru the Incas were even kinder. Now, Pizarro was not only greedy, but he was also very deceitful, and he made believe to the Incas that he was their friend; but all the time that he was taking their beautiful presents, he was learning about the country, so that he could come back in a little while with a bigger army and rob and murder them.

And, in a few years, Pizarro *did* come back with a big army. This time he had two hundred men and thirty horses and a great many guns. The Incas in all their lives had never seen a horse, and had never seen people killed with guns; so Pizarro knew that they would be very much frightened when they saw his men on horses, and saw the guns that killed with bullets. And they *were* afraid. Wherever Pizarro and his soldiers went, the Incas lost their courage. When they saw a man on a horse, they thought that it was all one animal, half man and half horse; and so frightened were they, that Pizarro came to one city that was quite empty, for all the people had run away in fear of the cruel Spaniards who were half men and half horses.

Yet I do not think that Pizarro would have conquered Peru if he had fought fair. There were so many soldiers among the Incas that they seemed to spring up everywhere; but Pizarro was very crafty, and he thought out a very clever, cruel plot. He made believe he was a friend to the Inca, who was the great King of all these people, and he invited him on a visit. Then when the Inca came to visit Pizarro, that wicked man had him arrested and cast into prison, and all the Indians who were with the Inca were killed or driven away.

Now, the Inca was a very brave young man, but he did not want to be killed. He knew that when he was dead, his soldiers would lose their courage. After a while, he noticed that Pizarro was very greedy for gold; so he said to him, "If you will let me go free, Pizarro, I will fill up this room with gold, and it will all be yours."

The greedy old Pizarro was very happy over this, for he always wanted gold. Now, I do not know why any man should want so very much gold, because you cannot eat it or drink it or wear it. But Pizarro was greedy, as greedy as any old man in all the world, and so he promised the Inca to let him go free if he filled up the room with gold. The Inca sent for his messengers, and day after day the servants of the Inca came carrying great heaps of gold. At last, after six months, the room was almost filled to the ceiling; but even then the treacherous Pizarro did not keep his word. He made believe that the Inca was trying to raise an army against the Spaniards (which I think he would have had a right to do if he wanted to, for, after all, the country belonged to him and not to the cruel Spaniards); so, instead of letting the brave Inca go home, as he had promised, the cruel Pizarro told him he must die, and the very same day he had the Inca put to death.

After that, the greedy, deceitful Pizarro got more gold, and more gold, and always more and more and more. Wherever he went he made the people give him money. He really ruled the country, although he pretended to the Indians that he did not, and he ruled it very cruelly indeed, and every day he became richer.

But after all, the money he got did not do him any good. He was now one of the richest men in all the world. But nobody loved him, and I think that in his secret heart Pizarro was not very happy. Every day the savage old man became more greedy and more wicked and more cruel, until not only did the Indians fear him and hate him, but the Spaniards hated him even more. There was a man named Almagro, who had once been his friend; but Pizarro cheated him, too, and then murdered him. Well, at last, one day, the son of this Almagro, a young man named Diego, went to Pizarro's palace with some of his friends. "You have killed my father," cried Diego; "now it is your turn." The cruel old Pizarro, though he was seventy years old, fought bravely to the end; but he was stabbed over and over again, and at last he fell dead at the feet of Diego.

And thus ended the life of the brave, wicked Pizarro, the swineherd who wanted a castle. He became one of the richest men in all the world and conquered a nation; yet sometimes I think he would have been happier if he had always remained till the end of his days a poor swineherd.

THE NOBLE WHO BECAME A SLAVE

During all this time, while Cortez was fighting in Mexico and Pizarro was making his plans to go to Peru, there lived in Spain a great noble, named Cabeza de Vaca. This man was always talking about America. He could tell you about Christopher Columbus and his great voyages, and about Balboa and Cortez, and all the other Spaniards who had gone to America. Whenever any ship came back from that land, De Vaca was always anxious to hear all the news.

Now, as the years went on, De Vaca thought that he, too, would like to go to America. He said to himself, "If Cortez can find gold and riches in that country, why cannot I?" Besides, he believed, like so many others at that time, that somehow or other he could find a way through America to the Indies. The Indies were supposed to be very rich, and De Vaca thought it was a country with more cities than the stars of the heavens. He had been told that each of these cities had more people in it than you could count in a year, and he also thought that all these people had gold and diamonds and rubies, and would give them to you for little glass beads. "If I only can find a way to this place," he said to himself, "I shall be the richest man in the world. I shall be as great as the great King."

So, because he wished to find gold in America and because he wanted to find a way to another land which, he thought, was even richer than America, De Vaca sailed away to the West. He was not the captain of the fleet; but, being a rich lord, he was, of course, very important. West the ships sailed, until one bright day in Spring they landed at Tampa Bay, in Florida.

Now, Cabeza de Vaca and the Spaniards with him were not the first men who had come to Florida. This part of the country had been found about sixteen years earlier by a rich Spaniard named Ponce de Leon; and the story of how Ponce de Leon came to find Florida is so interesting that I must tell you about it.

Ponce de Leon was one of the brave men who had sailed with Columbus across the great ocean, and afterwards he had been made Governor of an island called Porto Rico. He was rich, and famous, and powerful; but he was not happy, because he was growing old and he wanted to be young.

In those days the people believed that old men could grow young again, just as they believed many other things that we now know are very foolish. One day an Indian came to the great Ponce de Leon and said to him, "If you will go to the islands of the West you will find there a magic fountain. Bathe your hands in the fountain and drink the waters, and as soon as you have done so, a strange thing will happen. Your white beard will become black; your dim eyes will grow clear; your weak, thin legs will grow strong and stout again."

Ponce de Leon loved youth more than he loved money or power or anything else in the world. So he made up his mind to sail away on a ship and find the magic fountain. I do not know whether he wanted only to get young himself, or whether he wanted all the people in the world to bathe, so that no one would ever grow old and no one would ever die. It would have been very strange, I think, if Ponce de Leon had found the fountain. There would never have been any old people any more, and your grandfather would have been as young as you are.

Well, there wasn't a place in all the islands of the West that Ponce de Leon did not visit to find the magic fountain. Every day the old man would put his hands under some little fountain, and then watch to see whether his hair would grow black and his legs strong again. It never happened, and, for one, I do not believe that there ever was such a magic fountain. Well, one Easter morning, while sailing around looking for islands, where the magic fountain might be hidden by trees, Ponce de Leon saw a beautiful new land, the most beautiful land he had ever seen. There were wonderful green palms that never died, and on the ground were flowers of all colors, red and yellow and blue and purple. The air was soft and warm, and high up in the trees the birds sang so sweetly that it almost made the old De Leon weep. "It is Paradise," he said; "here I shall surely find my youth."

He called the country Florida, which is the name it still bears, and he looked everywhere for the magic fountain, of which he had been told by the Indian. But he did not find it at that time, nor did he find it later, though he came back again, with many men who wished to make homes in Florida. The Indians were very unfriendly; they did not want the Spaniards to land, so there was a battle between the Spaniards and the Indians and De Leon was shot. The arrow had been dipped in poison and the wound got worse and worse, and in a short time Ponce de Leon died.

So it happened that the old man who looked for youth found death instead. Yet, to-day, Florida is a beautiful land, where the flowers still grow and the birds still sing, and many people go there from all over our country to bathe in the wonderful salt water and the warm sunshine, and here they get health and strength, though, of course, they do not get what Ponce de Leon looked for—youth everlasting.

Perhaps the Spanish noble, Cabeza de Vaca, thought of the poor Ponce de Leon when, so many years after, he and his companions landed in Florida. "What will happen to us?" he said to himself. "Will we find what we want, gold and a way to the Indies, or will we too die from hunger and sickness and the poisoned arrows of the Indians?"

When the Spaniards landed from their ships, they found that the Indians were quite as unfriendly as they had been to Ponce de Leon. So the Spanish noble, De Vaca, told the captain, whose name was Narvaez, that he thought it would be safer to stay near the ships. The Indians had told Narvaez that there was gold in the country towards the West, near the mountains. Narvaez wanted gold right away, so he and his men didn't listen to De Vaca, but began their weary march inland.

Now, this march was much longer and harder and more dangerous than any of the Spaniards had thought when they started. There were no roads or even paths, and they had to cut their way through great forests, where the trees and bushes grew so thick that you could hardly tell where you were going. Often they lost their way in swamps. Their feet sank into the water, and they had to ask each other's help so that they would not sink into the swamp and die. The sun, too, was broiling hot, and the mosquitoes and insects bit them all day and all night, so that often they cried out with pain and could not sleep.

Besides, every day the Indians were more and more unfriendly. This was the Spaniards' own fault. They had burned some Indian chiefs, whom they had found in a little village, and all the other Indians hated the Spaniards and thought them very wicked. They called them white devils. Now, the Indians knew of a good way through the swamps and the forests, but they would not tell the Spaniards, because of the Indian chiefs whom the Spaniards had burned. So Narvaez and De Vaca and the men who were with them had to fight their way through the great swamps. Some poor fellows died of sickness, and all were hungry and tired. So you can well believe that they were glad to reach at last a little Indian village.

The Spaniards expected to find gold here, but there was hardly any gold in all the village. They did find a little corn and enough food to keep them from dying; but even with this they were little better off than before. The Indians were their enemies, and whenever a Spaniard walked away from the village he was sure to be killed with an arrow. Even when the Spaniards led their horses to water, they were shot at by the Indians, who were hidden behind trees. At last things became so bad that the Spaniards had to go back to their boats by the sea. It was a hard march. They could only get food from the Indians by fighting for it, and many Spaniards were shot, and many others fell sick and died from the bad water in the swamps. They had to go on, because the Indians would kill any who stayed behind. So they marched, and marched, and marched, day after day, and day after day, losing men all the time, until at last they reached the great sea.

But it wasn't Tampa Bay, where they had left their ships many weeks before, nor was the coast like any they had ever seen before. There was no life anywhere on all the great water, and there was no human being on all the miles of hot, white sand that stretched away as far as the eye could see. The soldiers lost their courage. "We shall never get home," they cried in despair. "We shall die on this terrible sea-coast," and some of the great, strong, bearded men threw themselves on the sands and cried as though their hearts would break.

Well, after a while they picked up courage. No matter how bad things look, a brave man never gives up hope. They knew that they were hundreds of miles west of Tampa Bay, but they remembered that there were some few Spaniards living near the place where they were. So De Vaca and the others made up their minds to build boats in which they might sail to the other Spaniards. Well, it is not easy to build ships when you have no sails, and no tools, and no pitch, and no ropes; but with patience you can do almost anything. So the Spaniards cut down trees for wood, made rope out of the hair of their horses' tails and manes, and used their shirts for sails. Month after month they worked, living on horse-meat and shell-fish and a little corn which they took from the Indians.

At last the boats were finished and they sailed away. Up and down the coast they went, always hunting for the Spaniards who lived nearby, and all the time things grew worse and worse with them. They were hungry and sick and frozen to the bone. For days the sun beat down on them, burning their skin, and then the cold shock gave them chills and fever. At last a great storm came, that drove their boats apart and threw them up against the rocks.

The boat on which De Vaca sailed landed on a little island, and the little band of soldiers would surely have died of hunger if the Indians had not been very kind. The Indians built large fires for the half-drowned men, and gave them hot food and drink, and when some other boats appeared like little specks far away in the distance, they threw more wood on the fires so that the smoke would rise in clouds and guide these ships also to the shore.

Here the tired Spaniards stayed for many months; but most of them did not live long. One after another they died, until only De Vaca and three others were alive. These four were all who were left of the bold men who had sailed for Florida a year before.

But the troubles of the brave De Vaca and his three tired men were not yet over. They could not stay long on the island with the good Indians, so one fine morning they said good-by to their new friends, and made their way to the West. It is a great wonder to me that they did not all die, for their troubles and dangers were great. Sometimes the Indians were kind to them, and gave them food and a place to sleep; but often they were very cruel, and once they kept De Vaca and his men locked up, and made them work as slaves.

You can imagine, perhaps, how hard it was for Cabeza de Vaca, who was a noble and a great man in his own country, to have to be a slave in a little Indian village. In Spain there were always people to wait on him, and whenever he wanted anything, he called and a servant came to ask what he wanted. But here in the little Indian village, where all the people were half naked, he had to work in the fields and dig, and cut wood and carry water, and do whatever else his master told him. Yet, I wonder, did De Vaca ever think of the thousands of Indians who had been made slaves by the Spaniards? Slavery is always wrong, and it was just as wrong to have Indian slaves as to have black slaves, or white slaves, or slaves of any kind.

So this great noble had to work for the Indians, but it was not for long. In a short time, the Indians saw that their slave was wiser than they were; he could teach them many things, and he could cure them when they were sick. So they were good to him and treated him as a chief, and after a while they let him and his three men go free.

Now that De Vaca and his three men were free, they started on their journey again. They went on day after day, week after week, month after month, and year after year. It was six years, six long years, that they walked on and on over deserts and thick forests, crossing deadly swamps and great, wide rivers. Often they had nothing to eat but nuts and roots, and as their clothes had worn out, they froze in winter and almost burned in summer. Many a time they wanted to lie down and die; but, being brave men, they never quite gave up hope. So they kept on. Then one day through the great forest they caught sight of the sea, and they were so happy that they wept tears of joy; and here they found that they were among their own people again. For the first time in six years they saw white faces once more; for the first time in six years they heard men speaking their own beautiful language, the Spanish language, which they loved so dearly.

You can well imagine how glad everybody was to see them. The tired but happy Cabeza de Vaca had to tell his story over and over again—all the wonderful adventures he had had since he landed in Tampa Bay, of the great rivers and swamps he had crossed, and of the sufferings he had passed through. And where do you think he was? He was far to the West, way out upon the Gulf of California, near the great Pacific Ocean. Cabeza de Vaca had walked across America.

It is true that De Vaca never found the things he came to America to find; for not always did men find gold and glory like Cortez and Pizarro. But De Vaca was happy and satisfied. When he sailed away back to his own home in Spain, he had no gold to take with him, but he was happy, happy to be with his own people once more, happy that he no longer had to be a slave to the Indians in America.

How De Soto Came To
The Father Of Waters

In the olden days, while the bold Columbus was sailing across the ocean, there lived in a gray, mossy castle in Spain a young lad named Ferdinand de Soto. This Ferdinand was a very lonely boy. He had no father and no mother, and there were no other boys with whom he could play. All he could do was to watch the birds flying in the green woods near the castle, and listen to their sweet songs. Sometimes, in the long, beautiful afternoons, he would go out walking with his faithful dog, or ride on top of his big black horse, that the boy had known and loved ever since he was a little baby.

Ferdinand did not go to school. There weren't many schools in those days and only the very rich could go; and Ferdinand, though he lived in a castle, was very poor. But he did learn how to ride on a horse and how to fence with a sword. His servant taught him these things. This servant was a good, strong old man, with eyes as black as coal and hair and beard as white as snow. Soon the young Ferdinand learned so well that he could fence better than his teacher, and as for horses, Ferdinand could ride horses that the old man was afraid to mount.

One day there came to the castle a very rich nobleman, named Don Pedro. He looked at the handsome young Ferdinand and was very much pleased with him. Ferdinand was very polite and had good manners, so at last Don Pedro said to him, "You seem like a very fine lad. How would you like to come to my palace and learn to read and write and become a great soldier like your father used to be?" "I should like it very much," replied the young Ferdinand. "I should like to learn many things and then be a soldier; and when I am a man I wish to go to America like Columbus." "Very well," said Don Pedro; "come with me and live in my palace."

You can imagine how happy the young Ferdinand was to leave the gloomy old castle to go with Don Pedro. And he was still happier when he got there; for the rich Don Pedro had a daughter named Isabella. This Isabella was as beautiful as the day and as good as she was beautiful. The two children liked each other, and in the lonely afternoons they played many games while the sun cast its long shadows on the green grass. Ferdinand now had lessons. He learned to read and to write; he went to a great school where they taught him many wonderful things, and every day he grew taller and stronger, until at last his birthday came around again and he was nineteen years old.

Then a strange thing happened. The young Isabella, too, had grown up to be a beautiful girl, with wonderful deep gray eyes, and red lips that curved like a bow, and her hair was as black as the darkest night. Ferdinand loved Isabella very tenderly, and Isabella loved Ferdinand, and they wanted to marry and live happily ever afterwards. But Don Pedro was away in America and they had to wait until he came back.

At last Don Pedro came home, and Ferdinand went up to him and said, "Don Pedro, you have been very good to me. You have brought me up like your own son. Now I am a man and I love your daughter, Isabella. May I have her as my wife?"

Now, Don Pedro was a greedy man, and he wanted his daughter to marry a great, rich lord, and not a poor young boy like Ferdinand. So he said, "No, I will not let you marry my daughter. You have taken my food, but you may not take my child." So Ferdinand was sad and did not know what to do, for he loved Isabella very dearly; but he could not marry her against her father's wishes.

Then Don Pedro thought of a very clever plan. He said to himself, "If the young Ferdinand and the young Isabella live here in my castle, their love will grow until it knows no bounds; and perhaps some day when I am away serving my King, these young people will get married. That will never do. But if I can get Ferdinand away, then Isabella will forget him, and will marry a great, rich lord and live in a beautiful, big castle."

So the clever Don Pedro said to Ferdinand, "You have always wanted to be a soldier and go to America like the great Christopher Columbus. Now is your time. You are a man, and can gain honor and gold for yourself, and new countries for your King. You must not think of Isabella; you must think of America."

The words of the clever Don Pedro moved the heart of the

brave young lad. "You are right, Don Pedro," he answered; "I will go to America."

I think that Ferdinand must have been very sad when he had spoken these words; for little did he know whether, in all his life, he would ever again look upon the sweet, beautiful face of Isabella. Perhaps on his way to America the little ship would strike a rock or go down in a storm, and Ferdinand would be drowned. Or perhaps the Indians would kill him, or he would die of a fever, or would be cast into prison, with nothing to eat or drink but bread and water, and the rats would squeak, and the day would be as dark as the night. Perhaps he would be thrown into such a prison by some wicked man and never be set free again. And even if he came back after many hard years and many great perils, he might find that Isabella had married and forgotten all about him; so you may well believe that Ferdinand, brave young man as he was, wept bitter tears when he said good-by to the fair Isabella.

And yet Ferdinand was anxious to go. All the brave young Spaniards wanted to go to America to fight the Indians, to teach them about God, to find gold for themselves and new countries for the King. Every now and then some young man would come back from America with gold, and silver, and pearls, and rubies, and beautiful, wonderful birds, and strange things that no man had ever set eyes on before; and many were the stories about the red men who lived in the beautiful land of America.

Well, at last the ship was ready and Ferdinand sailed away, and for fifteen long years he stayed in America. I cannot begin to tell you of all the wonderful sights he saw there, or of the many bold deeds that he did. Of all the brave men who had gone to America, none was braver than Ferdinand de Soto. After a while he met the Spanish General, Pizarro, who was going to Peru to conquer that country. Pizarro told De Soto about Peru and the Incas, of their wonderful temples and palaces, and how rich they were with all their gold and silver. "I am going to Peru to conquer that country," he said to De Soto, "and I want you to come with me because you are such a brave man."

Now, when Pizarro. said these words to De Soto and told him of all the dangers he would meet in that new land, the young Ferdinand was not afraid. He loved danger as he loved the beautiful Isabella whom he had left in Spain. "I will go with you, Pizarro," said Ferdinand, "and I will be a brave and true soldier." And so, during all that great war against the Incas of Peru, Ferdinand fought bravely by the side of Pizarro, the wisest and the bravest of all the men in that army.

When Peru was conquered, and after many other great adventures, Ferdinand returned to Spain. Fifteen years had passed since he had left. Now he was no longer a poor boy, but a rich and powerful man, and everybody respected him because of his wise words and brave deeds. You may be sure that Ferdinand was very happy to see once more the beautiful country in which he was born. However much you may travel, you are always happy when at last you come back to your own home. So it was with Ferdinand. He almost cried with joy when he saw again the old, mossy castle where he had played as a boy. There were the same old trees, the same long, dusty road where he used to ride upon his great black horse; but most happy of all was Ferdinand when he saw again the beautiful Isabella. She was more lovely than ever. Her father, the clever Don Pedro, was now dead, and during all of these long years the beautiful Isabella had loved the young Ferdinand. She had been very sad because Ferdinand was away, but she never forgot him; and when the great lords of Spain had come to her and asked her to marry them, she always shook her head and spoke sadly. "No, my good lord," she answered; "I love the young Ferdinand de Soto who fights for his King in the land of America. I shall wait until he comes for me."

So they were married, and all the great lords and ladies who were invited to the wedding said they had never seen so handsome a couple. There were plenty of cakes and wine for all the people who came, and there was a table where the poor could sit down and eat as much as they wished. Everybody laughed and cried for joy. Then Ferdinand took his beautiful wife to a great palace in Seville, and there they lived so happily that the days flew by like minutes, and even the King envied them because they were so happy.

The brave Ferdinand was very good to his beautiful wife. He bought for her all that her heart could desire. So it happened that he spent all the gold and silver that he had brought with him from America. Then, one day, Ferdinand said to his wife, "I shall go to America again to bring you more gold and more silver and all the beautiful things that are found in that country." Ferdinand said this to make his wife happy; but the beautiful Isabella was not happy. "I was so sad when you went away the last time," she said, "I cannot bear to have you leave me again. Let me, I pray you, go with you and share your dangers."

So the good Ferdinand de Soto kissed his brave wife and told her she might go with him; and many young lords of Spain wanted to go also. They all knew how bold and true and wise Ferdinand was; so the ships were filled with young nobles, all dressed in bright-colored clothes. After a long journey, the ships came to the island of Hispaniola, where there were many Spaniards. Here Ferdinand told Isabella to wait for him. "There are many dangers where I go," he said; "but soon I will come back with gold and silver and all that the heart can desire." Little did Ferdinand know when he kissed his wife good-by that he would never again see her in all this world. Boldly he sailed to the land of Florida. Here he found many wonderful things, but nowhere did he find the great mines of gold and silver that Cortez had seen in Mexico and Pizarro in Peru. The Indians told him that gold and silver could be found in the great wild country to the West; so Ferdinand and his little army marched toward the West. Every day they moved further and further away from their home, and further and further away from the lonely Isabella, who waited on the island. Everywhere they looked for gold, but the Indians always pointed toward the West, where the sun sets. Always they said to the Spaniards, "Go West; go far West into the wild, wild country and there you will find gold."

In their long, hard march, the brave Ferdinand de Soto and his little army had many adventures. Sometimes the

Indians were friendly and would sit down with the white men about the fire and smoke their long pipes. This was a sign among the Indians to show that they were friends with the white men. But sometimes the Indians were not friendly and fought with the Spaniards. I do not blame these Indians for fighting with De Soto. Before De Soto had come to this land, there had been other Spaniards there, and these men had been very, very cruel. They had killed many Indians and thrown their pretty little babies into the river, and one day they took the Indian chief and cut his nose off. Some of the Indians thought that all Spaniards were cruel and wicked, and so they fought against De Soto and killed many of his men. Then other misfortunes befell De Soto. There were many great rivers to cross and there were no boats; so De Soto made canoes out of the trunks of trees and moved his little band of soldiers over on these. But sometimes the boats were unsafe, and horses and men were drowned. Then, too, many of the men died of fever because they had to go through great swamps, where no white men had ever been before, and where you sank into the ground up to your waist. Sometimes there was not enough food, and many of the men grew sick and died; so the soldiers grew afraid and begged to be taken home. But the bold De Soto said, "No; we are all brave men and we must never turn back."

Then there happened one of the greatest things in all the world. De Soto had come to America to find gold and he did not find it; but he found what was much greater, a mighty river. This river was the greatest in all America.

"IT WAS FERDINAND DE SOTO WHO FIRST FOUND THIS GREAT RIVER,
WHO FIRST CAME TO THE FATHER OF WATERS."

it was so large and great that the Indians called it the Mississippi, which means in their language the Father of Waters. This river has become the great water way of America; cities have grown up on it, boats have gone up and down its wide waters, and more good has come from it than from many barrels of gold. And it was Ferdinand de Soto who first found this river, who first came to the Father of Waters.

When De Soto saw this Mississippi River, there were no boats on it and no cities near it. It was just a great, wide river, gleaming in the sun, stretching out its wide arms toward the north and the south. But De Soto was happy. He loved the river as he loved the beautiful Isabella, who waited for him so many, many miles away. And now Ferdinand was willing to turn back. The Indians were not at all friendly, and his army was very little and very weak. Many of the soldiers were sick from the fever; so sadly De Soto turned his back on the great river and started his march home.

But before he had gone many miles, the great Ferdinand de Soto fell sick. Every day he grew worse, and every day he longed to see his beautiful Isabella and the wonderful Mississippi River that he had found. But the fever grew worse and worse, and at last the brave Ferdinand de Soto died.

The sad soldiers buried him in the forest and then started homewards. But before they had gone many steps, one of the soldiers, who was very clever, thought of a plan. "If the Indians find De Soto's grave," he said, "they will know that our brave leader is dead. Then they will no longer fear to attack us. Therefore, let us bury him in the great river that he loved so well, so that no man can find his grave." And this they did. They took up his body and put it into the hollow of a great, heavy tree, and in the dead of night they placed it in the river and let it sink. This was almost four hundred years ago. Yet, perhaps, even to-day, at the bottom of the great Mississippi River, there lies the body of the brave Ferdinand de Soto, who, among all white men, was the first to come to the Father of Waters.

THE BOY WHO LOVED THE SEA

More than three hundred years ago, in a little town on the shores of the sea, there lived an English lad whose name was Walter Raleigh. This Walter was a very bright, happy boy, active and brave. He loved all kinds of sports. He loved to run and fight and play. He loved to breathe in the cool, fresh air, as every evening he ran along the lonely country roads; but most of all he loved the sea. Every day the young Walter could be found in the blue water, swimming near the shore, or rowing in a boat, or sailing before the wind. He loved the sea, and was not afraid of it, even in the stormiest weather.

Now, Walter was not the only English boy who loved the sea. All the little English lads loved it. The English at this time did not live in great cities as they do to-day. Many of them, like Walter Raleigh, lived in little towns and villages right on the shores of the sea. They could look at the water every day when it was blue and quiet and the sky was clear, and also when the sea was rough and angry and storms broke out from the clouds overhead. There were many bold fishermen in those days, and these fishermen would sometimes take the

little lads out with them in their boats; and so it happened
that at this time many of the English boys knew a great deal
about the sea and became good sailors.

The young Walter used to listen to long stories about the
great English sailors who were taking their ships to all the
seas but the stories he loved most to hear were of two brave
young Englishmen, named Francis Drake and John Hawkins.
These sailors hated the Spaniards, who were then the strongest
and most cruel people in the world. So these brave English
sailors used to fight against the cruel Spaniards and lay in
wait to capture their vessels and all the gold and silver that
was in them. Sometimes I think the English sailors were just
as cruel as the Spaniards with whom they fought; but they
were very brave, these English sailors were, and when the
young Walter heard about them, he, too, wanted to go to sea
and fight the Spaniards and take their gold.

But the time had not yet come. The young Walter was
only fourteen years old, and he had much yet to learn. A boy
should learn many things before he becomes a man. So the
young Walter was sent to the great University of Oxford,
where he was taught a great many things. He used to study
out of big books, that were so heavy that a boy could hardly
carry them. It was a very beautiful place, this Oxford, and
Walter met there many lads from all over England. They told
him wonderful stories about the great men of England, the
soldiers and sailors, the poets and the great lords who lived
in London and saw the Queen every day, and helped to rule
the kingdom. Walter longed to grow up to be a lord, so he,
too, could see the Queen and help to rule the kingdom.

Now, Walter loved to study; but, more than anything else, he wanted to go out into the great world and be a man. So at seventeen he left the beautiful school at Oxford and went to France, where a great war was going on. He fought for six years, doing many brave acts and becoming a great soldier. Then he went to Holland and helped the people of that country to fight against the Spaniards; and everywhere he went the people loved him, because he was so brave and handsome and witty.

But Raleigh loved the sea even more than he loved fighting, and when he was twenty-six years of age, he left the army and went on a ship to America. He wanted to go to Newfoundland, which is an island many miles north of this country, because he thought he could sail further and find a river or strait that would lead right through America to the Pacific Ocean. If he could find such a river or strait, then he could sail right through America to the Indies, and do what Columbus tried to do so many years before.

Well, there isn't any such strait in all America, and so Raleigh never could have found it; but he did not even get the chance. The Spaniards saw his little vessels and sailed after him, and he lost one of his ships and his other ships were damaged; so the brave Raleigh had to come home again.

Then there happened a little thing that made Walter Raleigh the most famous man in all England. One day, while he was in London, he saw the Queen walking along the street. Now the Queen, whose name was Elizabeth, was very proud and very fond of clothes. She had over a thousand dresses, and many of these were embroidered with beautiful jewels. I do not know how many shoes and slippers and silk stockings she had, but I do know that she had very many. Now, just as Walter looked up, he saw that the Queen stopped in front of a muddy place in the street. She did not want to get her new shoes wet. The great lords who were with the Queen looked worried. They did not know what to do; but young Walter sprang forward, took off his handsome cloak, the most beautiful cloak he had, and, kneeling down before the queen, spread the cloak on the muddy spot in the road, so that she could walk on without getting her shoes dirty.

Well, the Queen was very much pleased. She smiled at the handsome young man at her feet, and, telling him to rise, asked, "What is your name, young man?" "May it please your majesty," he replied, bowing very low, "my name is Walter Raleigh." "Well, Master Raleigh," replied the Queen, "you have done a very gracious act. Ask of me what you will and you may have it."

Now, this was the way in which queens spoke in those days when they were pleased with anything you did; and sometimes the man would ask for a suit of armor, and sometimes for a horse, and sometimes for a hundred pieces of gold. But Walter Raleigh asked for none of these.

"May it please your majesty," he said, "if I may have anything I wish, then I ask for the cloak upon which your majesty has just deigned to step." By this he meant that it was a great honor for the Queen to walk on his cloak.

Now, Queen Elizabeth was very much surprised.

"Why, Master Raleigh," she answered, "the cloak is not mine to give; it is yours and has always been yours."

"Not so," replied Walter Raleigh; "not so, your majesty. The cloak was mine until your royal foot touched it, but in that moment it became yours. And this is what I ask of your majesty, that you give to me my cloak that I may always look on it and remember this day."

So the Queen gave Raleigh his cloak, but she gave him many other things besides. She made him a knight, which was something that all men wanted to be, and she let him have lands and gold and many beautiful things. She made it a law that no man in all England could sell broadcloth or wines except only Walter Raleigh, which made the young man even richer than before.

Those were good days for Walter Raleigh, or, as he was now called, Sir Walter Raleigh. He was the greatest man in all England. His clothes were the finest in the kingdom. Even the band around his hat had pearls on it, and he wore diamonds and rubies and beautiful feathers, and the white ribbons that tied his shoes had beautiful, gleaming jewels sewed all over them. He even had a suit of armor that was made all of silver. Indeed, he had so many things that I cannot remember them all.

Of course, Raleigh loved to be a great lord among the English and help to rule the kingdom, but he loved the sea even more. "Now, that I am rich," he said, "I wish to buy ships and sail to America. There I can find a new land for England, and in after years Englishmen will bless the name of Walter Raleigh."

So Sir Walter Raleigh went to the Queen and told her of his plan. "Yes," said the Queen, "I shall be glad if you send your

"WALTER SPRANG FORWARD AND SPREAD HIS HANDSOME CLOAK ON THE MUDDY SPOT."

ships to America and find new lands for England; but you cannot go yourself, Sir Walter. I want you to stay in England and help me rule the kingdom."

She said this because she was very fond of Sir Walter, and was afraid he might die on the long journey, or be killed by the Indians in America. Now, the Queen's words made Sir Walter very sad. He wanted to go with the ships to the new land, because ever since he was a little boy he had loved the sea; but he had to do as the Queen said, so the ships sailed without him.

Now these ships went to America and came home again. The sailors brought back with them a string of white, gleaming pearls, skins of strange animals, and two Indians, to show Englishmen what red men looked like. They told Sir Walter wonderful stories of the beauty of the country, and when Sir Walter heard the stories of the sailors, he wanted to go to this new land more than ever; so the next year he sent out more ships. Now, on these second ships went one hundred brave men, who, when they saw the new land, called it Virginia. The Indians told Ralph Lane, the Governor of this colony, many strange stories. They told him of a beautiful city, back in the forest, where the walls were made of pearl, and where there was gold and silver in the streets. Now, we know that there was no such city; but the Governor believed the Indians, and instead of planting corn for the winter, he and his men searched and searched for the walls of pearl. Everything went badly with the little colony. There was not enough food to eat, and many of the men starved to death. The Indians, too, became unfriendly, though at first they had been very kind to the white men. I will tell you why they changed. One day an Indian stole a silver cup from an Englishman, and instead of punishing the thief, the white men burned all the corn that all the Indians had planted, and set fire to all their houses, till the whole village was in ashes; so the poor Indians had nothing to eat, and no place to sleep, and I, for one, don't blame them for not being friendly to the white men.

Every day things grew worse, and at last the little band of Englishmen went back to their own country. They had not found gold or silver, but they had found what was much better, tobacco, potatoes and corn. These things had never been known in England before, though to-day all the people in Europe use them just as the Americans do. Sir Walter himself liked tobacco very much, and, being a grown man, he used to smoke every day out of a great, long pipe. One day a very funny thing happened. He had hired a new servant, a man who had never seen tobacco in all his life. Sir Walter sent him out to bring in a great pitcher of beer, and when he came back he saw smoke coming out of his master's mouth and nose, and he thought that he must be on fire. So what do you think he did? He poured the pitcher of beer over Sir Walter's head to put out the fire. Of course the fire did not go out, but all of Sir Walter's clothes were spoiled; but Sir Walter had more clothes, and so he only laughed.

The ships which Sir Walter had sent to America all came back, but he did not lose hope, and after a while he sent out a third colony to the new land. In this colony there were one hundred and fifty men, seventeen women, and eleven little children, and Captain John White was their Governor. But the people of this colony, too, were cruel to the Indians, and so, of course, the Indians were unfriendly to them.

After a little while all their food gave out, and as the Indians would not give them corn, they asked Captain White to go to England and come back with more food. Now, Captain White did not want to go on this long journey. His little granddaughter, the first English child ever born in America, was only a few weeks old, and Captain White didn't wish to leave her; but if he did not go back, the people would die of hunger. So one fine day he set sail for England.

Now, at this time, there was a great war going on in England against the Spaniards, and all English ships had to be used in the fight; so Captain White's vessels were taken from him, and he could not go back to his little grand-daughter, Virginia Dare, nor to the men and women and children he had left in Virginia. It was three years before he could get ships to cross the great ocean, and when he did make the long journey, the people he had left so long ago had all been lost. What became of them no man ever knew. Perhaps they died of hunger or were killed by the Indians. It was all so many, many years ago, and the people that were alive then are now all dead; so we shall never know what did become of the little band whom Sir Walter Raleigh sent to America, or of the dear little baby, Virginia Dare.

After a few years, Raleigh, who still loved the sea, got the Queen to let him leave England. This made him very happy, and, buying some ships, he sailed across the ocean to South America. Here he landed in a country called Guiana, not a rich country, but where there were many Indians. Of course, these Indians told him wonderful stories, and, of course, these stories were not true. A tribe of Indians, they said, who lived up the river, were so rich that they sprinkled gold dust on their bodies; and back in the forest were other tribes who had eyes in their shoulders and mouths in their chests. Raleigh believed these foolish stories, because in those days people were not so wise as they are to-day, and so he sailed up the great river in search of these riches.

Well, as there was no gold or wonderful city, of course, Sir Walter Raleigh could not find them, though he hunted a long time, and so, after a few months, he went back to England a very sad man.

Now, as Sir Walter Raleigh grew older, this is what happened. Queen Elizabeth, as queens sometimes do, grew tired of her friend, and one day poor Sir Walter was thrown into prison. Of course, the Queen let him out again, but, by this time, everyone had turned against him. Now, many men hated Sir Walter because of his great pride; so, when Queen Elizabeth died, and a new King, King James, ruled over England, the King heard many stories against Sir Walter. He believed these stories, and so, for the second time, Sir Walter was put in prison. Here he stayed for twelve sad years. That was a long time to stay in prison; but, I suppose, Sir Walter would have been there even longer had he not thought of a plan by which to get out.

You see, Sir Walter knew that King James was very fond of gold; so he sent a man to the King to say, "In South America is much gold. If your majesty will let me out of prison, I will go to that country, and after a short time will return to England with my ships full of gold." This plan pleased King James very much, so he let Sir Walter out of prison, and gave him ships, and sent him to South America. But we cannot always do what we promise to do; and though Sir Walter tried very hard, he could not find any gold in South America. Instead, he became very sick, and some great Spanish vessels, seeing how small his ships were, chased him, and forced him to return home. Poor Sir Walter Raleigh!—you may well believe that he was sad at the thought of meeting his angry King.

And the King *was* angry when he found that Sir Walter had not brought the promised gold. He threw him into prison, and then a little later ordered his head to be cut off. By this you see how very angry the King was.

Now, Sir Walter was always brave. He was brave as a little boy, brave as a soldier, and brave when he came to die. Touching the edge of the axe that was to cut off his head, he said, "This is a sharp medicine, but a sound cure for all diseases." By this he meant that after death his troubles would all be over.

And so they were. Though the cruel King James cut off the head of this brave man, he could not make people forget him. Even to-day we remember Sir Walter Raleigh. We have a city named Raleigh in memory of him, and in all parts of our country the children are told of the brave little English boy who loved the sea.

THE LITTLE RED PRINCESS
OF THE FOREST

This is the story of a princess—not a fairy princess with golden locks and long, silken gowns, but a real princess. *You* might have called her a savage if you had seen her running barefooted about in the forest, because she was just a little, black-haired Indian girl, who played with other little Indians in the woods of Virginia. Yet this little girl was a princess and her father was a king.

Now, the name of this princess was Pocahontas. It is a large name for such a little girl; and yet, though it is three hundred years since she lived, no one has forgotten her name. No one has forgotten the story of the beautiful red princess who lived in Virginia, and this is the reason why:

In those days Virginia was very different from what it is to-day. There were no cities, and railroads, and houses, and street cars; no theatres, or parks, or schools. There were no white people there at all. It was all a wild country, with great rivers, and forests where no roads led, and all the people—the men and women, the little boys and girls, even the tiny, dear little babies—were Indians.

Well, as the years went on, little Pocahontas had her twelfth birthday. She was so beautiful, and so very good and kind, that all the Indians loved her. The women embroidered her skirts with bright-colored porcupine quills, and with feathers and beads, and the men brought her presents of beautiful birds and little gray squirrels which they trapped in the forest. But the King, her father, loved her most. Whenever he came back from a journey, his first question was always, "Where is Pocahontas?" And then he patted her on the head and gave her some shells which the Indians used for money. There was nothing in the world that the King would not do for his little daughter.

Now, Pocahontas had never seen a white man. She thought that all men were red like her father and the other brave Indians with whom she lived. You see, there never had been any white men in her part of the country. The brave, cruel Spaniards had gone to Cuba and Florida and Mexico and countries to the south, and the French explorers, who were very brave too, had gone north to Canada and to the great St. Lawrence River. The English, to be sure, had sent men to Virginia, but they had only looked around the coast and had not gone into the forest. So Pocahontas and her father, King Powhatan, had never seen a white man in all their lives.

But one day the soldiers of the King brought into the village a prisoner, whose hands and feet were tied with thongs. This prisoner was a tall man, with light hair and blue eyes, and, what was even more wonderful, with skin as white as milk.

The Indians shook their tomahawks in front of his face, and made a motion with their long knives as though they were going to cut off his head, but the man only laughed and he did not show any fear. Now, the Indians like a brave man, and when their prisoner laughed at their knives, they thought he must be a very brave man indeed. And little Pocahontas, who was watching from the door of her father's wigwam, which is the Indian name for a little tent, thought him brave too. She liked this white man, who was not afraid of the tomahawks of the bravest warriors, and she was sorry when she saw how the thongs of deer-skin, with which he was bound, cut into his white skin; so she asked her father to have the Indians unbind their prisoner, and this they did.

Now, the name of this white man who laughed at the tomahawks was Captain John Smith. He was one of the bravest of all the brave Englishmen who came to America so long ago. He had been a soldier in England, and when he was very young had gone to fight against the Turks, who were making war on the Christians. The young John Smith was so very brave in this war that when the English wanted men to win the new country of Virginia for their good King James, they chose him for their captain.

I do not think that anybody ever had more trouble or ran into more danger than did this brave gentleman. It was not easy to cross the ocean in those days. The little sail-boats were often wrecked, and then there were cruel pirates who would catch sailors and throw them into the sea. And even when John Smith and his little band of men sailed up the James River in Virginia, and made the new city of Jamestown, their troubles were not over. They did not have enough to eat, and it was hard to get any food from the unfriendly Indians. Besides, the men who had come with Captain Smith were not used to work. They wanted to find gold and silver and become rich right away, and they did not want to plant corn, and build houses, and barns, and forts.

So you may well believe that Captain Smith had enough trouble. When his people did not have food and were hungry, and when some of them fell sick and died, as they did, then they all complained. They even cried to go home to England. They had much trouble with the Indians, too; and at last, as I told you before, Captain John Smith and some of his men were captured, and Smith was bound and taken to King Powhatan's village. So you can well believe that poor John Smith was very happy when, to please Pocahontas, the King ordered him to be untied.

Now, the Indians were curious to know all about the white men. They spent long hours in front of their wigwams listening to the strange stories of Captain Smith. He wrote a few words on a sheet of paper, and when the Indians saw how the white men in Jamestown could read these little black marks on the paper, they were filled with wonder, for the Indians had no schools, and could not read or write. "It is strange," they said, "our prisoner can talk to a man a hundred miles away. He must be a great chief and a friend of the gods." Then Captain Smith showed the Indians his compass. He told them that with this little needle he could never be lost in the forest; even where the woods were dense, he could find his way back to the camp-fire. Now, you and I know that the needle of a compass points always to the north; but the Indians did not know this, and they thought it was magic that told Captain John Smith the way. So they grew afraid of this white man; but Pocahontas was not afraid.

The days passed, till one morning the King, Powhatan, called his warriors together to see what they wished to do with their captive. They all sat around a great camp-fire, and each man smoked his long pipe. Pocahontas was not there, because no woman was allowed at these meetings; but you may be sure that she was very anxious to hear what they would do with the white man. After a while, one of the Indian chiefs—he was a very old man, with a great scar running across his forehead—spoke:

"I know it is the custom of our tribe, oh, King Powhatan, to kill the men who are taken in battle; but this man is not like other men. He is brave; he can talk to his friends a hundred miles away; he speaks with magic to the stars. So I say send him back to his people."

When the man with the scar had finished speaking, there was a low murmur, which showed that many of the Indians were pleased. But there were others who did not like Captain Smith and were afraid to keep him alive. A little old man, who was very thin, and had a very squeaky voice, arose and spoke:

"Oh, King Powhatan, it is not safe to let this man live. He is the friend of the devils, or how else could he talk with the stars, or by little marks speak to his friends a hundred miles away? Besides, it is the custom of our tribe that we kill all prisoners. Therefore, I say, oh, King, let the white man die."

And so it was agreed. I think that in his heart the good

King Powhatan would have liked to save Captain Smith, but he would not go against the wishes of his chiefs. You may well believe that Pocahontas was very sad when she heard that her friend must die. During the long summer days, when he had been a prisoner in the village, she had grown very fond of him. He had told her wonderful stories of England, the great country across the sea, and of the little white boys and girls who lived there, and of the schools they went to and the games they played; and now the man who had been so kind to her must die a cruel death, far from the country he loved.

All day she walked in the forest, trying to think of some plan by which she could save his life; but when night came and she returned sadly to camp, she had not yet thought of a plan. Now, as she neared the village, she met a young brave dressed in his war-paint. "Hurry, oh Princess," he said, "for the white man is to die at sundown."

Poor Pocahontas! She ran even faster than the young brave, and reached her father's wigwam just in time to see John Smith, bound hand and foot, stretched on the ground, his head resting on a big, flat stone. All the Indians made way for the Princess as she pushed her way to the front, and then, as a warrior raised a great club to dash out the Englishman's brains, she fell on her knees and threw her arms around his neck. If the club fell on Captain Smith, it must kill her too. From her knees she begged her father, the King, to give to her the life of the white man.

Powhatan and all the Indian chiefs loved a brave act. They looked at the little girl kneeling before them, ready to die to save her white friend. So the King said, "Let the white man go free." And the Indians all grunted, which meant that they, too, were really glad.

So John Smith rose from the ground a free man, and was sent with twelve Indians back to Jamestown. But this was not the only time that the little Red Princess saved the life of her friend. The Jamestown settlement was in danger of attacks by bad Indians, and more than once Pocahontas came through the great forest at night to warn Captain Smith that his enemies were coming. Then, too, she asked her father, the King, to give corn to the English, and often the little village would have starved but for the Little Red Princess of the Forest, who sent them corn.

One day, when Pocahontas came to Jamestown, she found that Captain Smith had gone back to England to be cured of a wound. This made her very sad, but she still went often to Jamestown to hear news of her friend. At last one day she was told that he was dead. After that the Little Red Princess stayed in the forest. She did not go then very often to the English village, though she still sent presents of corn to the white people.

But John Smith was not dead, and Pocahontas was to meet her good friend once more. Not in the great, silent forests was she to see him, nor yet in the little city of Jamestown, but in England, far across the sea. And this is how the Little Red Princess of the Forest happened to go to England.

In the village of Jamestown there lived a young Englishman named John Rolfe. Now Rolfe was not a prince, and in stories only the prince can marry the princess; but a real red princess is different from a fairy one, and so, after some years, Pocahontas and John Rolfe were married.

The wedding was in the little church at Jamestown, because

Pocahontas had become a Christian, and you may well believe that all the good Indians came to see their beautiful princess married.

Well, after some time, John Rolfe and his young wife crossed the ocean to England, and thus it was that in the great city of London Pocahontas met her old friend, John Smith, once more. You may well believe that she was glad to see him again after so many years, and that they had many happy times together. It soon happened that everyone in London was talking about Pocahontas. The London people had never seen a red princess before, especially a princess who had done so many brave deeds, and saved the lives of so many Englishmen. So all London wished to honor her. The King and the Queen sent for Pocahontas, and she was often at their court, where all the great lords and ladies loved her and gave her beautiful presents.

But at last the time came for John Rolfe to go back to Jamestown. Pocahontas was very sad at the thought of leaving England and all her kind English friends, and she was sad, too, because her little son, who had been born in England, must take the long, rough journey. But their plans were all made, and the good ship was ready to sail.

Then it was, at the last moment, that poor Pocahontas was taken ill. All the great doctors of London came to see her, but their medicines were of no use, and, after a few days of suffering, she died. John Rolfe buried her in England, among the white people there; but I like to think of her best in the great, silent woods of Virginia, where, for so long, she had lived with her Indian tribe, and where she was called Pocahontas, the Little Red Princess of the Forest.

THE ENGLISHMAN WHO
SAILED FOR THE DUTCH

This is the story of the man who started New York, the greatest city in all America. It all happened three hundred years ago, at a time when Sir Walter Raleigh was still in prison, and when the Little Red Princess of the Forest, way down in Virginia, was saving the life of Captain John Smith. And this is the way it happened:

In a little English village there lived a boy named Henry Hudson. This boy, like so many other English lads, loved the sea, and he always wanted to be a sailor. There were many games that Henry could play, but he was never really happy except when he was out on the ocean sailing his boat, and learning how to keep it safe in the wind and storm. He used to watch the rough fishermen as they steered their boats and cared for their sails in the rough weather, and soon there was nothing about a boat that the young Henry did not know just as well as a man.

Well, while Henry was still a boy, he went to sea to learn more about the great ocean. He did not run away secretly, but he went to the captain of a vessel and told him that he would work as a sailor for a few years without any pay, so that he could learn all about boats. The captain looked the young Henry over from head to foot, and he thought to himself, "Here is a fine, strong lad. He will make a good sailor." So he said to Henry, "You stay with me until you are twenty-one, and I will teach you everything about a ship and make a good sailor out of you."

So Henry Hudson stayed with the captain, and every day he learned more about the ways of the sea and how to handle a boat. He studied in books, too, and soon knew all about the seas of the world, and all the countries that any white man had ever visited. He was now a captain of a ship himself, and everybody was glad to sail on his boat, because they knew that Henry Hudson was a brave sailor, and was not afraid even in the roughest sea.

In those days there were great companies who sent out ships to all parts of the world to trade with the different nations. In England there was a company of this kind, called the Muscovy Company. Now, this company heard about the wise captain, Henry Hudson, and they wanted him to sail a ship for them and find out new countries, and sell English goods to the strange people he met in the new lands; so Hudson made several voyages for them. He sailed far north, and every day the weather got colder and colder; for, as everybody knows, if you go south it gets warmer, and if you go north it gets colder. Well, after a while it got so cold that the sailors almost froze. The ropes of the ships and even the sails were covered with ice, and in the sea the sailors saw great floating mountains of frozen snow. Now, these mountains are called icebergs, and they are very beautiful, especially when the sun shines upon them, and the white snow glistens, and the clear ice turns a wonderful shade of green.

But the icebergs, although very beautiful, are also very dangerous. They float around in the sea, and if they strike a ship, then that ship is broken to pieces the way a nut is crushed in a nut-cracker. So every day the voyage in the north became more dangerous, and some of Hudson's men wanted to go home; but their captain would not return. "I will not go back," he said, "until I have done what I was sent to do," and he kept on his voyage. So when Henry Hudson reached England, he had sailed further north than any man had sailed in all the world up to that time.

Now, when the people of Europe heard of how Hudson had sailed further north than anybody in all the world, they all wanted him to sail their ships. Holland, at this time, was a country of sailors, and here, too, was a company like the Muscovy Company, only it was called the Dutch East India Company. Well, the men who owned this company were always looking for brave captains; so, when they heard of Henry Hudson, they sent for him and said, "We are all Dutchmen and you are an Englishman; but, as you are a brave and a wise sailor, we want you to sail our ships for us." And they gave him money, and sent him off in a ship called the Half Moon, with twenty sailors, some of them Englishmen and some Dutchmen; and thus it was that the bold Englishman, Henry Hudson, sailed for the Dutch.

Again Hudson sailed towards the north, but this time it

HENRY HUDSON GOT MANY FURS FROM THE INDIANS AND
MADE THEM ALL HIS FRIENDS."

was colder even than before, and the sea was so full of ice that his sailors grew afraid, even more afraid than his first sailors had been. You see the ice was really *very, very* dangerous. If a boat got shut in the ice, you could not move it, no matter how hard you tried; and if it got caught between two great icebergs, it was squeezed until its masts and sides were broken to pieces. So I am not surprised that the sailors grew frightened, for I should have been frightened if I were there, and I think you would have been frightened too. And they *were* frightened. They said they would throw Hudson overboard unless he steered south; so Hudson had to tell the pilot to turn the boat, and he sailed south along the coast of America.

Now, I have told you before how in those days all sailors believed in a short cut between the Atlantic Ocean and the Pacific Ocean; so it is not strange that Hudson believed in this short cut, too, and wanted to find it. Besides, Captain Smith, who was a friend of Hudson, had told him that there was such a short cut. The name that was given to this short cut was the Northwest Passage, although nobody had ever seen it, and, in truth, there wasn't any to see. Well, as Hudson was sailing along the coast, he came to a great stream, which he thought must be the great Northwest Passage that all brave sailors were in search of; so he turned his boat and sailed up the river, which was really the Hudson River, the river that flows through the State of New York, and does not go anywhere near the Pacific Ocean. The water was clear and fresh, and the longer Hudson sailed, the shallower it became, until, after he had gone about a hundred miles, his boat could go no further, so he had to turn around once more and sail back. His men landed on the beautiful green banks of the river and rested from their hard journey.

So it was that the Hudson River was found by Henry Hudson, and the great city of New York was founded by Dutchmen. You see, though Henry Hudson was born in England, he sailed for the Dutch, and that gave the Dutch the right to all the land he found. Well, they liked this river, these home-loving Dutchmen, and they liked, too, its beautiful harbor, so they sent out from Holland ships with people to build houses and forts and trading stores for the Indians. Here they also gave the Indians hatchets and knives and little glass beads of many colors, and got from the red men soft, beautiful furs; and soon there was a little village here, which the Dutch called New Amsterdam, after their own city of Amsterdam in Holland. For over fifty years they held this little city, and then the English came and took it from them, and called it New York. And this is its name to-day, the name of the greatest city in all America, the city built upon the land which Henry Hudson found.

Let us return to Henry Hudson. He soon saw that this beautiful stream was nothing but a river, and not a short cut to the Pacific at all. He was sorry, of course; but anyway, he did a great deal. He got many furs from the Indians and made them all his friends. You see the Indians liked Hudson because he was good to them. He did not treat them cruelly as the Spaniards had done, and he did not try to rob them, or murder them, or make slaves of them; and the Indians never forgot this kindness, and from that time on they were friendly to all the Dutch who came to that part of the country.

At first the Indians did not know what to say or do to Hudson and the white men. Like the other Indians of our stories, they had never seen a ship or a white man before. Some of them thought that the ship was a great fish or an animal, and still others believed that it was a strange, new house that floated on the water. As for Hudson, they thought he was the *Manitou*, or Great Spirit, who was the god of the Indians, and they worshipped him in a very queer way. Gathering in a great circle, they danced around him all their queer Indian dances, because, being a great spirit, they thought that their dancing would please him.

Then Henry Hudson gave the Indians axes and shoes and stockings, but the red men did not know what to do with the gifts. They thought the heads of the axes and the shoes must be ornaments to be worn about the neck, and the stockings they used to put tobacco in and they hung them at their belts. Now, I think that shoes and stockings were very foolish gifts to make to the Indians, because everybody knows that they always wear moccasins; but the axes were a very *sensible* present. The Indians were pleased with these axes. They cut down trees and chopped wood for their fires, much more easily than before, when they had used their big hunting knives.

Well, the Indians certainly did like Hudson and Hudson liked the Indians; so one day the chief invited him in to dinner. It would not have been polite to refuse this invitation. You see, Hudson could not say that he had a "previous engagement," which is the way some people have of making excuses when they do not want to go anywhere. Anyway, Hudson really wanted to go. When he came to the wigwam, he found the chief seated on a mat on the ground. Hudson looked around for a chair; but, as there was none, he sat down on a mat too, and waited for what would come next. Then the food was served. It was in two big wooden bowls and of only one kind—a sort of stew, made up of pigeons and *dog* cooked together. Now, a dog isn't a *very* good thing to eat, at least we don't think it is; but the Indians thought this a very fine feast. Well, Hudson was polite, and he had such a good time at the dinner that the Indians were sorry when he sailed away.

I think that Henry Hudson wanted to come back again to the friendly Indians; but when he reached Europe, the English kept his vessel and made him stay in England. Hudson wanted to sail again for the Dutch, but his own people said, "No; you must sail for us. You must not find new lands for any country but England."

So the next year the brave Hudson sailed once more, and this time he sailed on an English ship. He took with him his own son, a young lad, and a man named Henry Green, and also a good many sailors. You will hear of this Henry Green again before this story is ended.

Far north Hudson steered the little vessel, and soon he came to a great bay which no white man had ever seen before, and which was afterwards called Hudson's Bay, because Hudson found it. Here it was very cold indeed, and every day it grew colder. The ice froze around the vessel, and for eight months the little ship could not move an inch. Food got scarce, and then, as always happens, the men were afraid of starving and longed to get home. As soon as the ice began to melt even a little, they begged Hudson to go back to England. "Do not stay in this cold land," they said, "where we shall surely freeze and starve to death." But Hudson would not do this. He believed that at last he was in the Northwest Passage, and would soon find the Pacific Ocean. "Be brave," he said, "for this ship shall not return to England until I find out about this bay." Perhaps these words of Hudson would have kept the men quiet if it had not been for the wicked Henry Green. Hudson had always been friendly to Green, but this wicked man was not grateful. Night and day he talked to the men until he got them to turn against their good captain. And they *did* turn against him in this way.

Hand and foot both Henry Hudson and his son were tied so tight that they could not get loose, and then, with seven sick men, they were put in a little boat and turned adrift in the great sea, while the wicked Henry Green and the other men sailed home to England. When they reached home, I am glad to say, these wicked men were all punished. They were put in prison, and a ship was sent to Hudson Bay to look for the brave Henry Hudson; but he was not found, and to this day no one knows what became of the little boat and of good Captain Hudson.

So I suppose that, left alone without food, he died there in the great, frozen sea. But who knows? There were many simple Dutch people who lived near New York, in the Catskill Mountains, who never believed that Hudson was dead. Whenever it thundered in the hills, these old men used to say, "Henry Hudson and his men are playing ninepins in the mountains."

THE FATHER OF NEW FRANCE

About three hundred years ago, there lived in France a man who wanted to find a new country. He loved France, its green fields and its cool forests, its rivers and quiet country roads, its cottages and its beautiful palaces; but what this man wanted was a New France, a country where Frenchmen could go and speak their own language and meet other Frenchmen.

This man's name was Samuel Champlain. Even as a little boy, when he played with other lads in the fields, he had this one plan—to find a new country for France. He knew that he could find this country in America, because America was so big; so he asked everybody he met to tell him what they knew about the great wild country beyond the sea.

He asked questions about the lakes of America, its rivers, its great forests and its wide plains. He asked questions about its gold and silver, its mines and fisheries, and the vegetables and fruits, and everything that grew there.

Now, in the little town in which Champlain grew up, there lived some fishermen who had been to America. They had not been in the southern lands, like Mexico, Florida and Peru, where the Spaniards had gone for gold. The Spaniards did not like the French, and they would not let a Frenchman live in the countries that belonged to them; so these bold fishermen of France sailed further north. They used to start in the first warm days of spring, in their little fishing boats, and sail all the way across the ocean to America. Here, in the quiet, silent waters, off the coasts of Maine and Newfoundland, they would fish all summer, and when the weather got cold, they would sail back with their fish to their little homes in France.

They were very brave men, I can tell you, these French fishermen. Sometime one of them would get caught in a storm, and his little boat would go down to the bottom of the cold sea. Then a poor woman in France would sit by the window waiting for her husband to return—waiting, waiting, waiting. And sometimes these fishermen would land on the shore in America, or sail their boats up the rivers. They told Champlain of the wonderful sights they had seen; of the wide rivers rushing down from the north; of the deep quiet of the beautiful forests; of the tall spruce and pine trees; of the clean, cold waters of the little lakes. They told how the naked Indians went about in light canoes, made of the bark of trees; how these Indians would carry their canoes on their backs from river to river and from lake to lake. They told Champlain of the beautiful brown and white furs that the Indians had—furs so soft and warm that any lady in France, even the Queen herself, would be happy to wear them.

When Champlain had heard all these stories, he became more eager than ever to make a new France in America. This cold country of the lakes and forests did not have gold and silver mines; but, after all, thought Champlain, "gold and silver are not the only things in the world." The Frenchmen who would live in this New France could get fish from the rivers, beautiful woods from the forests, and soft, warm furs from the Indians. Champlain dreamed of the, time when all this country would be filled with Frenchmen, living in beautiful new cities, and loving and obeying the King of France.

Now, Champlain was just the man to find a new country. He was very wise, and very, very brave. Of all the men who went to America, Spaniards and Frenchmen, Dutchmen and Englishmen, I do not think there was anyone braver than Champlain. When he was still very young, he had sailed in the French ships and had learned to be a good sailor and a plucky soldier. He had fought in many battles for his King, and no one could ever say that Samuel Champlain was a coward.

Then later, after he had left the army, Champlain went to the West Indies and to Mexico. Here he saw the lands that Columbus had found, the lands that Cortez had conquered, and he watched all that the Spaniards were doing in these soft, warm lands to the south.

But as I told you, the bold Champlain wished to find his new country, not in the warm lands to the south, but in the cold countries to the north. So, after a while, he joined a little band of Frenchmen who were going to the great country which is now called Canada. Now, these Frenchmen with whom Champlain went were good, kind men. They did not kill the Indians nor rob them, as, I am sorry to say, so many other white men did, but they loved the Indians. There was one man among them who was very, very kind. His name was

Poutrincourt. He had been a great lord in his own country, but he did not want to go back to his beautiful France. He lived peacefully and happily with the Indians, taught them new ways of farming and many other things of which they had never heard before. And the Indians loved the French lord as they did their own father. Even the little Indian children used to come in and out of his house whenever they liked, and lie on the ground while he ate his dinner; and every now and then he threw them raisins and nuts, which they caught in their little brown hands.

Now, this life was very beautiful; but Champlain was not happy. He wanted this great country of America to belong to France, and he wanted to learn all about its rivers and lakes and forests, so that the other people who would come later would know the way to go and the best places to live in. Across great forests he went, looking at rivers and islands and lakes, till at last he reached the mighty St. Lawrence River, where another Frenchman had been a hundred years before. Here Champlain stayed for several months, and then he returned to France.

But the next year, which was 1608, Champlain came back again to the St. Lawrence River. He began now to build a little city called Quebec, which was to be the great city of the new country; but even before his workmen were through putting up the first houses, there was trouble for good Champlain. Among the men whom he had brought with him from France, was a very wicked fellow named Duval. I do not know why Champlain let him come along, but I suppose that at first he did not know how wicked Duval really was. You see, many of the soldiers who first went to America were very cruel and very wicked. Anyway, this Duval made a plan with three other men to go to Champlain's bed while he slept. Then all the four men were to take Champlain's neck in their hands and squeeze it till he could not breathe, and so strangle him to death. It would have gone hard with Champlain if one of the men had not told him of this wicked plot. When Champlain heard it, he arrested the four men. He then had the wicked Duval hanged, and the other three men he sent back to France to be punished.

But this was not the last of Champlain's troubles. A great sickness called scurvy broke out among the men who were with him. Of the twenty-eight men, twenty died, and only eight were left to bury the dead. Even these eight men were sick, and every day they came to Champlain and begged him to take them back to France. "Do you not remember," they said; "do you not remember how warm and sunny and beautiful it is at home; how the blue grapes hang in heavy bunches on the green vines; how the lovely women smile with joy, and the little children play about our knees and beg us for stories? Let us go back to our beautiful France and to our wives and children." But Champlain told them to be brave and patient; so they waited, and in the spring their courage was rewarded. More ships came with brave Frenchmen, and these ships were loaded down with food; so all the men with Champlain were again happy.

Champlain had learned that it was best to be kind to the Indians, and so it happened that all the Indians near

Quebec were his friends. Now, one day Champlain heard of a great lake to the south, and he wanted to go there to find out all about it. So he asked the friendly Indians to take him; but they shook their heads. "We cannot go there in peace," they said, "because of the Five Nations." "Who are these Five Nations?" asked Champlain. Then the friendly Indians answered him quickly: "They are our enemies, these Five Nations. They are Indian tribes who kill us when they can, and whom we kill when we can. We are always at war. "But," they told Champlain, "though we cannot go to the great lake in peace, we are going there in war. We are going to fight the Five Nations. Come with us, you and your men and your guns, and fight with us against these peoples."

So Champlain and two of his men went with the friendly Indians to fight the Five Nations. There were sixty Indians in all, and they traveled in light canoes, going down the rivers that emptied into the Great Lake. The Indians in front always held their bows in their hands, ready to shoot if they should see any of the warriors of the Five Nations, and those in the back canoes were always looking around for animals, so that they could shoot them and cook them, so that the little army would have enough food. Every night they sent a few canoes ahead to watch out for the enemy.

At last, one evening, as Champlain and his men were canoeing down the lake, they met the Indians of the Five Nations. There were two hundred Indians in this army; but the sixty friendly Indians were not afraid, because they had Champlain with them. "When the Five Nations see the guns of the Frenchmen," said the chiefs among themselves, "and hear them speak noise and fire and death, they will be so afraid that they will run away and we will win the battle."

It was too late to fight that night, so both little armies waited until the sun rose on the lake the next morning. During all the long hours they stayed near each other, and in the darkness they each called the others cowards. They made a great noise, I can tell you.

Well, the fight began the next morning, and then the army of the Five Nations had a great surprise. The first thing they saw was a white man in gleaming armor, who held a gun in his hands, and had a gleaming sword in his belt. The Indians shot their arrows at this white man, but the arrows did not do any more harm than if they had been shot at a rock. Then Champlain aimed his gun and shot bullets, and two of the chiefs of the Five Nations fell down dead. Two other Frenchmen shot bullets and more chiefs fell dead. Now, the Five Nations had never seen men killed in this way before. They could not see the bullets that went so fast through the air, and they thought that the white men had killed their chiefs with a noise; so the army of the Five Nations grew very much afraid. One of the Indians began to run, then another, then another, and soon their whole army was running away. The Indians who were with Champlain ran after them, shooting them with their arrows, killing and catching very many. I think that both sides were very cruel, and it seems to me sometimes that Champlain, though he was a brave man and a very wise man, would have done better if he had kept out of all their quarrels; for, from that day, the Five Nations were always

"CHAMPLAIN CAME BACK TO THE ST. LAWRENCE RIVER AND
BEGAN TO BUILD A LITTLE CITY CALLED QUEBEC."

the enemies of the French, and would never let the French go to the south, where they wanted to go.

After this, came busy years for the brave Samuel Champlain. He had found his new country for France, and every year he traveled over it and learned more about it. He traded with the Indians for their beautiful furs and sent them to France, where the fine ladies of the Court wore them in the winter. Champlain sent a young Frenchman to study the Indian languages, so that Champlain could talk to them in their own way, and he sent an Indian to France to learn to speak French.

But Champlain was too brave to stay always in Quebec, and so every now and then he would go on a great trip. Once he went north to find a great salt sea that a Frenchman had told him about. It was one of the hardest and most dangerous trips that a man ever took. There were great swamps, where Champlain sank to his waist; and deep forests, where the bushes and brushwood were so thick and dense that he had to cut his way with a great knife before taking a step. And all these hardships were useless, for there really wasn't any great salt sea; so, of course, they never found it.

Then Champlain went on a second long journey to the west. He traveled with the friendly Indians for many weeks, till at last they came upon the town of the Five Nations. You would have been surprised to see that town. It was not like other cities, with streets, and stores, and brick houses, and electric cars. It was just a few plain, long, one-story houses, as big as theatres. In these houses were a lot of little rooms, and in each room a family of Indians. Around the town were four rows of stakes, like telegraph poles, and the Indians stood behind these poles when they shot their arrows.

This time the Indians who were with Champlain were beaten in the fight, because they would not do as the Frenchman told them. Even Champlain himself was shot twice in the leg, and the Indians had to carry him away in a basket that they fastened to their backs. You see, they were friends of Champlain, and they did not want him to be caught and killed by the Indians of the Five Nations.

That was a hard winter for Champlain. The Indians who were friendly to him wanted him to stay with them, and when he asked for a guide to show him the way back to his home in Quebec, they would not let him go. You see, Champlain did not know this country as well as the Indians did, and he was afraid of getting lost in the forest; but the Indians treated him well, and when the spring came around again they took him home to his city of Quebec.

After this, Champlain worked day and night to build up his new country. He tried very hard to make it pleasant for the people who lived in Quebec, and always tried to get more Frenchmen to come from France and live in the new country. Every year he took the long journey across the ocean and told everybody there of the wonderful land of America. Of all the things in the world, what Champlain most wanted was to make this new France even greater and more beautiful than the old France.

I think that if Champlain had not been a very patient man, he would have many a time given up Quebec and gone back to France to lead a peaceful, quiet life. Often things went very bad indeed. New people did not cross the ocean as fast as Champlain wanted them to, and those who did come grumbled and quarreled. Often, too, the food gave out and the people got sick and many starved. But Champlain, though he was now a pretty old man, would never give up. Once some English warships sailed into the harbor and asked Champlain to give up the city to them. The brave Frenchman had hardly any soldiers; but he said, "No; I will never give up my city of New France. As long as I have a man or a bullet left, I will never give up the city of Quebec." And after a while, the English captain became frightened because he thought that Champlain might have a big army, and so he sailed away; but the next year three more English vessels sailed up the harbor, and as this time Champlain had only sixteen half-starved men, he had to surrender. But England did not long keep the city. It was handed back to France, and Champlain was again sent out to Quebec as commander over the little town.

So Samuel Champlain, the boy who had dreamed of New France, now went back once more to that country; but his days were almost over. He became very ill, and, after lying in bed for more than two months, he died an old man, at the age of sixty-eight years.

Many, many years later, there was a great war between France and England, and after the war was over the whole country of New France was given to England. The English changed the name of the country to Canada; but even now there are more than a million people living there who speak French, and who are the children of the children of the children for many generations, of the men who lived with

Champlain. And even now, after three hundred years, these Frenchmen, and other people in Canada, and people all over the world for that matter, revere the name of the great and good Champlain, and call him, as they used to call him so long ago, "The Father of New France."

THE FRIENDS OF THE INDIANS

Many, many years ago, two Frenchmen, traveling through a new, wild forest country, came upon a cross that was all covered with flowers. There were no white men in all this country, and so the Frenchmen wondered who had put the cross there, and who had placed the flowers on it; but later they learned that the Indians in this part of the country had laid the flowers on the cross. Then the Frenchmen knew that these Indians were friends, because everywhere the French went they carried the cross, and taught the Indians, who loved them, to place flowers on it.

Now, these two Frenchmen were very good men. They treated the Indians kindly, and the Indians, who liked to be treated kindly, were also good to the Frenchmen. There is a very good lesson in all this. If you want people to be good to you, then you must always be kind to them.

Now, all the Frenchmen who came to America knew this, and from the first they were kind to the Indians. The Spaniards had been very harsh. They had killed the red men or made slaves of them, and sometimes the Indians had been cruelly beaten until they died. They had been tortured, too; hung up by their fingers and toes; roasted over a hot fire; starved, and even chased with great, fierce blood-hounds. So I am not surprised that the Indians did not love the Spaniards.

Now, the English and Dutch who came to America were not quite so cruel as the Spaniards, but sometimes they, too, treated the Indians harshly. For a very little wrong they would shoot an Indian or burn down a whole Indian village. Besides, they were very proud, and thought that the red men were only savages, and they did not want to have anything to do with them; and this, I may tell you, is a very bad way to act and think, if you want people to like you and help you.

The Frenchmen who came to America acted much more wisely. They really loved the Indians, and often lived with them in their poor little villages. Some of the Frenchmen had been great lords in their own country. They had had beautiful castles, with fine, big rooms, and gold and silver and wonderful carpets. They had had many servants to wait on them, and everything in the world that they wanted. Yet these very men were not too proud to sleep on the ground in the hut of an Indian, or share with him a meal of corn and dried meat. They hunted with the Indians; they fished with them, they smoked their pipes with them, and Indians and Frenchmen sat around the roaring camp-fire and talked together, or looked up in silence at the bright little stars. Wherever the Frenchmen went, they put up little chapels, and here Frenchmen and Indians kneeled down side by side and prayed to the good God. The French priest would baptize the little red children, and when they grew old enough to understand, he would teach them about God and the Bible.

Some of the Indians became Christians, and hung flowers on the little crosses which the Frenchmen built all over the country. And so it was that when our two Frenchmen saw the flowers on the cross, they rejoiced and were glad, because they knew that even in this wild country, far away from all white men, they were with friends.

Now, these men were not only very good, but they were also very brave. One of them was named Louis Joliet. He had been sent by the King of France to find out some good way to the Pacific Ocean. The other was Father Marquette, a French priest, as brave a man as any soldier. This Father Marquette had lived with the Indians many, many years. He knew their languages and all their customs, and the Indians loved him and called him their friend.

Well, it was not an easy thing that these brave Frenchmen were trying to do. No white man had ever been in all this country before. It was much pleasanter staying in Quebec, the city which good Champlain, the Father of New France, had founded; but Joliet and good Father Marquette were not afraid of danger. They sailed down the St. Lawrence River into the Great Lakes, and then on and on and on, day after day, and day after day, until at last they reached Lake Michigan. I think this part of their journey must have been the most pleasant. The weather was warm, the Indians they met were friendly, and now and then they would come across some Frenchman who was living out in the wild country, trapping animals for their furs or trading with the Indians; and sometimes they would meet a good French priest, who had come this great way to teach the Indians about God.

Well, at last they left the last Frenchman and the last wooden cross, and started down a narrow but beautiful river that they believed flowed into the Mississippi. The little river was so choked with rice that grew wild along its banks that the boats found it hard to move. Here their guides left them, and then for a week they drifted slowly, slowly down the river, till at last, with cries of joy, they came to the Mississippi.

Now, this Mississippi River is the greatest river in America, and one of the greatest rivers in all the world. It was the same river that De Soto had found so many, many years before, when the Indians had told him that its name was the Father of Waters. Now, you see, whatever country owned the Mississippi River, the great river that flowed from little streams all the way down to where it emptied into the great, great sea, that country would own all the land along its banks, and so would be the greatest country in America. This was why Joliet and Father Marquette wanted to sail all the way down the river, so that all the land on its banks might belong to France. Besides, they thought that perhaps it flowed into the Pacific Ocean. You see, Joliet and Father Marquette had no good maps, and they did not know, as you and I know, that the Mississippi River flowed not west into the Pacific Ocean, but south into the Gulf of Mexico.

When the two brave Frenchmen reached the Mississippi River, they were a little afraid of the Indians who lived along its banks. Perhaps these Indians would be their enemies and would kill them; so they no longer left their canoes at night and slept on the banks about a roaring camp-fire. They feared that the sharp eyes of unfriendly Indians might see the smoke, and that they might come and cut off their scalps while they slept; so they tied their canoes to the shore and they rolled themselves up in blankets, so as to be ready to wake in a minute and paddle away. They also made one of their men stay awake all night to watch for the red men; but for eight days there was not an Indian in sight.

On the ninth day they saw a path leading up from the river, and they knew that this path must go to an Indian village. Joliet and Father Marquette did not know whether these Indians were friendly or not; but they were both brave men. Maybe their hearts beat a little faster, as they thought that, perhaps, the Indians would kill them; but, anyway, they did not show any fear as they walked up the path to the village. Well, after all, the Indians were friendly. The chief came forward with hands raised above his head, which was always a sign of friendship with the Indians. Then other red men waved the long pipe of peace, which was the same as though they had said, "Let us be friends, oh, white men!" The two Frenchmen were invited to take dinner, and the chief told them stories about the Great River and about the other Indians that lived along its banks. And at last, when Joliet and Father Marquette said good-by, all the Indians went with them as far as the river, and the Indian chief gave them a present, which was better than gold, or silver, or diamonds, or rubies.

Now, I suppose you will want to know what was this present that was better than gold, or silver, or diamonds, or rubies. Well, I will tell you; it was a pipe. Not a stale old pipe, such as a man carries in his pocket, but the calumet, the pipe of peace. Wherever Joliet and Father Marquette went, all they had to do was to show this calumet, or pipe of peace, and every Indian knew that the great chief was the good friend of these white men; and many times this pipe saved the lives of the two brave Frenchmen.

Well, wherever they went, Joliet and Father Marquette showed the calumet of the great Indian chief, and then the other Indians were friendly too. And these two Frenchmen were so good and brave that the Indians liked them for their own sakes; so down the river they sailed, past big forests and beautiful, rolling prairies, until one day they saw a wide, yellow river that flowed into the Mississippi. This was the Missouri, a great, yellow, roaring river, and if they had time, I think the two Frenchmen would have sailed up it; but they could not stop. So day after day they sailed on down, down, down the Mississippi. I think that they must have had a good time of it, seeing a new country all the while; but they did not go the whole way. When they had gone many hundreds of miles, they were told stories of some very cruel Indians who lived in the south. The friendly Indians said to them, "If you fall into the hands of these bad Indians, they will surely tie you to a pole and burn you alive; and if you escape, perhaps the Spaniards will catch you, and they are as wicked as the others."

So Joliet and Father Marquette talked it over for a long time, and at last they thought it would be wiser to go back. Slowly they sailed up the Mississippi River, and then across the country to the Great Lakes, and back the same way they had come. On the way home they saw graceful, white swans, with long, beautiful necks, swimming on the little silver lakes, and in the dark, green forests were cattle, and goats, and beautiful brown deer, with wonderful spreading horns. At last they reached Quebec, and all the people in the town wanted to hear of the great adventures and lucky escapes of Joliet and Father Marquette.

Now, there was a brave man named La Salle, who heard these stories from the mouth of Joliet. This La Salle was a very great man in France. His family were nobles and were very rich, and young La Salle, whose first name was Robert, had been well brought up, and had been taught many things. He was so good that he even became a priest, and everybody said that Robert La Salle was a very good and a very wise man.

But Robert La Salle wanted to go to America, not only to find new lands, but also to find what so many others had tried to find, a new way to the Pacific Ocean. So he gave up being a priest and went to the great, new country of America.

La Salle was not only a wise man, but one who thought a great deal, and now he thought of a new plan. This plan was to build little French forts, very little but very strong, all the way along the Great Lakes and the Mississippi River; and at the mouth of the Mississippi he planned a great, great fort. He wanted to put French soldiers in these forts, so that the whole river and all the country around would belong to France. When this was done, Frenchmen could go every-where to get furs, and soon little cities could be built, and there would be a great, strong, New France in America. So the dream of Champlain would come true.

Now, the first thing La Salle had to do was to sail down the great Mississippi and find the best places for his little forts and trading posts; and this was not an easy thing to do. In those days it was a long and hard journey from Quebec to the mouth of the Great River, and La Salle tried many times before he succeeded. On the first trip his ship was wrecked in a great storm and nearly everything was lost. Then he had no food, and had to sail back miles and miles and miles to get bread and meat. Later, his money gave out, and he had to wait until he had sold enough furs to buy a new ship. And then, when his men tried to sail on the lakes, the wind blew against them, and many times they had to sleep on the icy ground, with nothing but the sky over them. Often and often they had no food at all but a few handfuls of corn.

But the worst trouble that La Salle had was with his men. They did not want to do much work, and they were always complaining because the journey was so hard and because they had nothing to eat. Now, they knew very well before they started that it would not be easy, and so I, for one, think that they ought not to have complained; but so it is with people. Some, like La Salle's men, will grumble and grumble over every little thing, while others will bear all sorts of hardship and never say a word.

Now, there were with La Salle two men who never complained. One was his faithful French friend, Tonti, and another faithful friend was an Indian. These two men, one a Frenchman and one an Indian, loved La Salle and did whatever he asked. The Indian knew the forest. He could find his way through the great, thick trees even in the dark; so La Salle

"THE INDIANS LOVED THE BRAVE FATHER MARQUETTE, AND
CALLED HIM THEIR FRIEND."

took him as his guide. When everybody else was tired and cross, this good Indian was as brave and as patient as ever. This was because he loved La Salle, and because La Salle was always kind to all Indians.

Well, all the time the troubles of La Salle grew worse and worse. Sometimes the little streams were filled with ice, so that the canoes had to be moved on sledges, and sometimes these brave men had to wade for miles in water up to their waists. Of course, the brambles and thorns tore their clothing to rags, and when it grew cold, their clothes froze as hard as ice. Then they had to stop and build a fire before they could go any further.

I am sure these were times when even the brave heart of La Salle almost broke, but not once did he give up. Again and again he tried, day after day, till at last, after years of disappointment, La Salle reached the mouth of the Mississippi River. His patience and perseverance were finally rewarded. It was in February, over two hundred years ago, that the Father of Waters and all the country nearby was given by La Salle to the King of France.

You can imagine the joy of La Salle when at last he reached the end of his long journey. He put up a cross on the banks of the river. Then he asked all his men to kneel down and pray. Then it was that he named the new country Louisiana, in honor of King Louis, and, in a loud voice, called out that from that time on all the land should belong to France.

And for many years the great country of the Mississippi *did* belong to France. But later, much later, when the grandchildren of the men who had been with La Salle were all dead, a new country grew up in America—our country, the United States. And to us the French sold all this great country of the Mississippi. Yet the name of Louisiana is still the name of one of our States, and even to-day all Americans think of La Salle as a great and good man who did well for his country.

For all his good deeds La Salle was not rewarded as he should have been. Two years after he had found the mouth of the Mississippi River, he came back again with four ships and two hundred and eighty men. This time he wanted to build the city and fort that he had planned so many years before; but the captain of these vessels was a very stupid and a very jealous man. He took La Salle to the wrong place instead of to the mouth of the Mississippi, and when La Salle wanted him to sail again and try once more to find the mouth of the river, this evil man would not do so; so La Salle started by land. Now he had no map, and it was much further than he thought. Then, too, there were many hardships, and his men grumbled and grumbled, and would not do as he said. And at last two of the men, who were very wicked, hid behind trees, and when La Salle was walking to the camp, they shot him dead.

And that was the end of Robert La Salle, the man who found the mouth of the Mississippi, and who was one of the true, good and great friends of the Indians.

WHAT CAME OF IT ALL

And now my stories are ended. What wonderful stories they are! How strange and how true!

As I finished my last story, I closed my eyes, and it seemed to me that I saw again all those brave men who had come from the East to explore our America. I saw them all—noble and swineherd, priest and soldier, Spaniard and Frenchman, and Englishman and Dutchman. I saw the wise Columbus following the Queen from place to place, begging her to let him sail to the Indies. And again I saw him, after he had found America, when he was an old man, poor, sick and forgotten. And so, too, I saw the others—the wicked Balboa, the brave Henry Hudson, the good Father Marquette, who loved the Indians and was loved by them.

How strangely it all happened! These bold men searched for one thing and found another. Columbus looked for the Indies and found America; De Soto hunted for gold and came to the Mississippi River, and Ponce de Leon wanted a fountain of youth, so that he might drink the waters and never die, and instead of youth and life he found Florida and death. And so it was with the others. The unfortunate Henry Hudson never thought of the great city of New York, which was to grow up on his river; he only thought of a short cut to the Pacific Ocean. And the wicked Balboa, who hid in a barrel, did not think that he would be the first man to look upon the great ocean; but all he wanted was to get away from the men who had lent him money. So strangely did it all happen!

Yes, they were strange men and they led strange lives. Up and down they went, sometimes rich, sometimes poor, but always bold and daring. A man who had nothing in all the world would stumble upon a great empire and become rich and famous in the eyes of all men. Think of Cortez, who came out of prison to conquer all of Mexico, and who became so rich that he did not know what to do with his money, though at last he died poor and unhappy! And think of Pizarro, the barefooted, bareheaded swineherd, who became one of the greatest and richest and wickedest men in all the world! How strange Cortez must have seemed to the Aztecs, who had never before seen a white man, nor a horse, nor a gun, nor a house that sailed on the sea! And how strange the greedy Pizarro must have looked to the Incas, and how strange and curious the Incas and their wonderful country must have seemed to Pizarro!

Just so strange and wonderful were the things that happened to the other explorers. There was the nobleman, De Vaca, who became a slave to the wild Indians. Then there was bold Captain Smith, whose life was saved by the Little Red Princess of the Forest; and stranger still, this same little girl, who had saved his life in Virginia, saw him again in London, and this time she was a Christian and an Englishman's wife, and the friend of the King and Queen of all England. It was all very, very strange.

I wish that I could really see all these great men—the wise Columbus, who sailed new seas and found America; the patient Champlain, the good Father of New France; the bold La Salle, who sailed down the Mississippi River; the faithful Henry Hudson, the brave De Soto, and all the others. Yes, I should like to meet them, to shake their hands, to hear from their own lips their wonderful stories; but this cannot be.

All of these things happened hundreds of years ago, long before I was born, and all the men and all the women, all the Kings, and Queens, and nobles, and sailors, and soldiers, and priests, and Indian chiefs—all are dead.

And now you will ask me what came of it all. Well, that is another story, or rather, I should say, many stories. Many brave men came to America, and many brave men lived here, and strange and wonderful things happened; but the end of it all was that a new country arose in America—the United States, and you and I and all other Americans have this good land for our country.

And so we Americans, who live in the country that Columbus found, and the others explored and conquered, should always remember those brave men who risked their lives so many, many years ago; and for this reason we, who love America, should be grateful to them all, but especially to the one who first pointed out the way—to the bold sailor who crossed an unknown sea, the good, wise Christopher Columbus, the man who found America.

THE END.